GET MAITLAND

GET MAITLAND

JAMES PATRICK HUNT

FIVE STAR
A part of Gale, Cengage Learning

GALE
CENGAGE Learning·

Detroit • New York • San Francisco • New Haven, Conn • Waterville, Maine • London

GALE
CENGAGE Learning

LIBRARY OF CONGRESS CATALOGING-IN-PUBLICATION DATA

Hunt, James Patrick, 1964–
    Get Maitland / James Patrick Hunt. — 1st ed.
        p. cm.
    ISBN-13: 978-1-59414-965-8 (hardcover)
    ISBN-10: 1-59414-965-8 (hardcover)
    1. Maitland, Evan (Fictitious character)—Fiction. 2. Antique dealers—Fiction. 3. Americans—England—Fiction. 4. Organized crime—Fiction. 5. London (England)—Fiction. I. Title.
    PS3608.U577G48 2011
    813'.6—dc22   2010051992

First Edition. First Printing: April 2011.
Published in 2011 in conjunction with Tekno Books and Ed Gorman.

Printed in the United States of America
1 2 3 4 5 6 7 15 14 13 12 11

GET MAITLAND

ONE

Every Thursday night, Ian and Ken Shivers had supper at their mum's flat in South London. Their mother, Valerie, was no better or no worse than most English cooks. Usually she made them bangers and mash. Ian and Ken ate at a small table in the kitchen. The brothers would not discuss business in front of Ma. Valerie Shivers had heard talk of her sons' activities, had seen their pictures in the local dailies. The *Daily Mail* said her sons ran "the most dangerous mob in London." She didn't believe a word of it. Her boys were not gangsters or criminals. They weren't fiends. They were respectful and kind to her. They was gentlemen. Gentlemen in a way their father Frank never had been. The boys were the only good thing Frank had ever done for her.

Ian came first, Kenny about a year later. Before Ken started to put on the weight in his twenties, they were practically identical. When they were babies, Valerie dressed them in matching clothes. She told friends they looked like little bunny rabbits.

Neither one of them was in school past the age of fifteen. They seemed to attract trouble. Valerie never understood what the fuss was about. Ian and Ken fought at home as well, sometimes going at it like cats and dogs. Once, Ken knocked Ian to the ground and then jumped on his arm and broke it. Ian got up and broke Ken's nose. Valerie had to take them both to the hospital. No real harm done, though. Boys being boys. The hospital staff insisted on keeping Ian overnight. Kenny stayed with him, sleeping in a chair by Ian's bed. Valerie couldn't get Ken to leave. Indeed, Ken claimed that his arm hurt too. As Ian claimed that his nose felt broken.

It was strange, that. Each of them saying they felt the other's pain. But it seemed like they did. As they shared each other's thoughts.

They looked alike. But as the years passed, Valerie noticed some differences. Ian was a bit quicker, a little more clever. Ken was more volatile and quick tempered. Also, Ian liked girls. Valerie did not ask Ken what his preferences were. She chose to ignore the rumors. To her, Kenny had never seemed the least bit effeminate.

Now thirty-eight and thirty-seven, respectively, Ian and Ken remained very close to their mother. Yet they had never seemed, to Valerie, like children. They were her children, to be sure, but they had never *acted* like children. They had never laughed or seemed to take any pleasure in children's games. They had always seemed like formed adults, with dark and serious intentions. Even at a very young age, they were aware that others feared them. Even the older, bigger boys were afraid. For to pick a fight with one was to get in a fight with both. And the Shivers boys never backed down.

They ate their dinner in their tailored suits. Silk ties, gold rings and watches. Italian shoes, very black, shined daily.

At half eight, they put on their dark Crombie overcoats and left their mum's flat and walked outside to a '68 Jaguar MKII with red leather seats. The car belonged to Cliff Wilkinson, one of their men. The Shivers got into the backseat and Cliff Wilkinson drove the Jaguar away.

The car park was near Mayfair and it had one of those corkscrew drives going up the side. At eighteen past nine, the Jaguar came out of the eighth level of the corkscrew onto the flat lot and crept along until it found a parking space alongside a Range Rover. Cliff Wilkinson cut the motor and Ian and Ken got out.

They walked to the other side of the lot, past a battered Ford Cortina and one of the new German Minis. They came to the back side of the garage and took in the bleak, dark view of the city below them.

They heard a car door open. They looked and saw a man step out of a rental car, his arms raised in submission.

"I'm Dushane," the man said.

The man was in his fifties, short and of stocky build. He had a handlebar mustache that could only be an American's. His name was Lewis Dushane and he was a partner in the law offices of Dushane and Mansell, Chicago, Illinois. He had once sued a newspaper for writing that he was a "mob lawyer." He'd agreed to drop the suit when they publicly withdrew the comment.

Ian said, "Lewis Dushane?"

"Yeah."

"Welcome to England," Ian said. He was smiling.

"Thank you," Dushane said. And now he was next to the brothers. He decided that Ian had a good smile. Though not warm.

The other one was not smiling. Dushane did not offer to shake hands. He had been warned that the Shivers brothers did not like to be touched.

Ken said, "First time in London?"

"First time I've been here during winter," Dushane said. "Jesus, I didn't know how cold it could get here. I mean, we've got cold winters in Chicago. But there's something about the dampness here, it gets into your bones."

Ken Shivers said, "Hmmm."

"Well," Ian said, "you get used to it."

"And how's Eddie?"

Eddie Salvetti had taken over the Chicago syndicate after John Zanatelli had died of a heart attack in prison. Ken had visited Eddie on his one trip to the States. Since then, the U.S. government had prohibited Ken Shivers from returning. This had angered Ken—he didn't like being told where he could go. But he had never liked traveling that much anyway. He was never really happy or comfortable outside South London.

"He's good," Dushane said. "He sends his warm regards. To both of you. And he wanted me to personally express his regrets that he couldn't come here personally."

"Personally?" Ken asked, a glint of a smile on his face. Dushane felt his heart pounding.

"It's alright," Ian said. "Risky business, traveling."

Ken said, "Got something for us, then?"

Lewis Dushane looked from one brother to another. He hoped they didn't know how frightened he was by the dark, vacant looks in their eyes. *Get to it*, he thought. *Get it done and go.*

"Well," Dushane said, "as you may be aware, last week there was a theft in Chicago of approximately eight million dollars' worth of bearer bonds." Dushane looked at both of the men again, seeing if it would impress them. There was no change in their expressions.

A moment passed and Ian said, "I see. And what's that to us?"

"We want to dispose of them in Europe."

Ian said, "And?"

"And we need something else. We need forged registration certificates to make them negotiable."

"Right," Ian said. "Have you got a fixer?"

"Not in Europe," Dushane said. "And even if we did, Eddie said we should go through you."

Ken snorted.

"How generous," Ian said. "When?"

"He wants it done within seven days."

Ian shook his head. "It's not possible. We would need ten days, at least."

Below them a Fiat Abarth moved along the narrow road, slowed, then turned a corner.

"Okay," Dushane said. "We can do that. What's your cut?"

"Three-quarters," Ken said.

Dushane spoke without thinking. "Seventy five cents on the dollar? Are you nuts? We can't do that."

Then Dushane saw the dark eyes of Ken Shivers intensify, and his heart just about came to a stop. "Hey," Dushane said, "I'm sor—I didn't mean that."

"It's alright, Ken," Ian said. He put a hand on his brother's arm. "It's alright. He didn't mean nuffing. Right?"

"Right," Dushane said. "I only meant that I'm not authorized to accept that."

Ken said, "You tell Eddie—"

"I only meant—"

"You tell Eddie," Ken said, "that if he don't like the way we do business, he can take his fucking hands out of our Mayfair gambling clubs and invest his money somewhere else. Tell him if he's got the fucking balls to show his face here again, I'll fucking nail it to the floor."

"Ken," Ian said. "That's no way to talk to our American friends, is it?"

"Tell him that," Ken said, giving the American lawyer the coldest look he'd ever got in his life. Dushane tried to comfort himself with the thought that this man would let him live so he could deliver the message.

"Ken," Ian said, "take a fucking powder, will you? It's business."

11

Ken Shivers gave Dushane one more glare, time for Dushane to imagine himself being thrown over the wall and into the street. Then Ken walked off.

"I'm sorry, I—" Dushane said.

"Sod it," Ian said.

Dushane said, "Eddie said we can only pay fifty cents on the dollar. That's it. I'm sorry."

"Ken's not barmy," Ian said, "despite what you might think."

"I didn't mean—"

"But three quarters is what they charged in the old days."

"The market's changed."

"Not that much," Ian said. "Come on, Lewis, after all, you are using the services of our fixer."

"I can offer fifty-five."

"Kenny will go stark raving if I take anything less than sixty. Even I can't control him when he loses his head."

Ian returned to the Jaguar five minutes later. He closed the door and turned to his brother.

Ken said, "He agree to sixty?"

"Yeah."

Ken smiled. "Tosser," he said. Valerie always said he was a born actor.

They arrived at the Cardigan, one of their Mayfair gambling clubs, just after midnight. The Cardigan had a smoke-filled gaming room, a restaurant and a small bar. The restaurant was of a period: pink-shaded lamps and wood-paneled walls. Ian and Ken and Cliff Wilkinson sat at a table in the restaurant. They all ordered steaks. The manager came over to the table and paid his respects. Other patrons waved hello, one of them a well-known forward for Arsenal, another being last week's Page Three girl. The Shivers were London celebrities, appealing, charming characters to those who thought they understood them. The three men laughed and joked through the meal, celebrating the deal they had made, the money that was coming their way. Sixty percent of eight million dollars. Ian would contact the fixer and make the arrangements for the certificates. The whole thing wouldn't take more than a few days. When it was done, Ken would buy himself a new Rolls Royce. Ian would buy an engagement ring for Courtney, his girlfriend.

Ian decided now that he would not tell his brother about the engagement. Ken didn't like Courtney. Ken thought all women were smelly cows.

Now Ken called a cocktail waitress over, signaling her with one finger.

"Hello, luv," Ian said.

"Mr. Shivers," the girl said. Then said it again to Ken.

Ken asked, "Where's 'Arold?"

The girl's lip seemed to twitch. "I dunno," she said. "He was here earlier."

Ken put his hand on the girl's wrist, tightened it around. She said, "I don't, Mr. Shivers."

"You see him," Ken said, "you tell him I'd like a word with him."

"I will."

"And if I twig that you're lying for him, I'll tear your face off."

Tears now formed in the girl's eyes.

Ian said, "For Christ's sake, Ken, let her go. She's got work to do."

Ken released his grip on the waitress's wrist. She backed away and Ken said, "It's my personal business."

Ian gestured to the club around them and said, "And this is our business. She's not here to look out after one of your boys."

A few moments passed. The men at the table said nothing.

13

Then Ken held out his hand to Cliff Wilkinson and said, "Cliff, gimme the keys to the Jag."

Cliff Wilkinson prized his vintage Jaguar almost more than his life. He looked to Ian for some sort of reprieve. But Ian gave him nothing. Cliff handed the keys to Ken.

Ken pulled the Jag to a stop in front of a gay bar in Soho. He depressed the handbrake and left the Jag running while he went inside. Inside the chickens and old poofs parted ways for him and soon he found Harold sitting in a booth with a tall, shiny-skinned man of about thirty. The man had his hand between Harold's legs.

Harold had been Kenny's boy for about three weeks. Harold was nineteen, with thick dark hair and faintly Greek features. Another one of Ken's beauties.

The man with him was blond-haired and thin. He was drunk too and recently had moved to London from Manchester. Had he been a local, he might have been more careful. The blond man looked at Ken, sizing him up, his age and weight. He knew the look on Ken's face, having seen in it in other men and he thought he knew the situation, but he didn't know Ken Shivers.

The blond man said, "Oh, is this your dad then?" Being funny. He didn't see the boy next to him trembling.

"Oh, Christ," Harold said, scooting away from the blond man immediately.

Ken said to Harold, "Go outside, wait in the car."

"Yes, Ken."

Harold was out of the booth in a flash. He started to say something to Ken, but then seemed to think better of it and left. Ken stared at the blond man. The blond man looked back at him with a bored expression. Then the blond man smiled and said, "Good-looking boy, isn't he?"

Ken Shivers crooked a finger at the blond man, like a

schoolteacher. Ken said, "Come with me. I'd like a word with you."

"Whatever you say, sweetheart," the blond man said.

The blond man followed Ken to the bathroom. There was no one else inside. Ken shut the door behind them.

In the bathroom light, the blond man was able to see the dark, gypsy-like eyes of Ken Shivers. Then he felt fear. He decided he would explain himself to this person but before he could say anything Ken Shivers pulled out a stiletto and slashed it in a quick, downward arc. It opened the blond man's face up from his forehead to his chin. The blond man screamed and fell back and Ken slashed him again, this time cutting into his nose. The blond man went to the ground, screaming and crying. Ken crouched next to him and lifted his head up by the hair. The blond man saw the point of the stiletto inches from his eye.

Outside the bathroom door, muffled screams could be heard. No one moved to help.

In the bathroom, Ken said, "Next time, I'll slit your throat. Understand?" Ken shook the head by the hair. "Under*stand?*"

"Yes," the blond man croaked. "I understand."

Ken Shivers walked through the club. No one attempted to stop him. Glances were averted. One did not witness violence by the Shivers brothers.

Outside, a drunken patron said, "Hello, Ken." He noticed some blood on the gangster's hand and said, "Got a spot of blood there."

"Gardenin' accident," Ken said. Then he got into the Jaguar and drove away.

Two

Light snow came down in front of a brownstone mansion on Astor Street in Chicago. The snowflakes swirled under the cones of light of the streetlamps. Another flare of light came from the north as a car's engine could be heard. A silver 2001 BMW 740i Sport pulled up in front of the mansion. Evan Maitland got out of the BMW. A parking valet got into the BMW and drove it away.

In the foyer a servant took his overcoat. Maitland wore a blue suit. It was his best one. Bianca had asked him to wear a nice suit. She had told him it was important to make an appearance at this party. They were in the antique business, she reminded him, and she couldn't do all the schmoozing.

Maitland was self-conscious. He avoided these social events to the degree that he could. He used to be a cop and he retained some of the cop's defensive snobbishness. Bianca would say, "But you're not a cop anymore." She liked to remind him of that too.

Maitland was forty years old now. He was of average height and weight and, despite having lost a lung to a bullet, more or less physically fit. His hair was blond.

His business partner was Bianca Garibaldi. She was now separated from her husband.

Now Maitland saw her across the room in a conversation with a couple in their sixties. Bianca was wearing a black dress, tasteful and suited to her age, which was forty-five. *She does*

16

have style, Maitland thought. Men were becoming aware that she was separated from her husband. Would she remarry?

Now she turned her head and saw him. She smiled. Maitland smiled back. She cocked her head, half-mocking an appreciation for his suit. Maitland spread his hands apart in a self-deprecating gesture. She laughed back at him and motioned for him to join her.

She touched him lightly on the arm and introduced him to the couple and he joined the conversation. Maitland found them to be pleasant people, though perhaps a little dull.

Maitland felt his arm grasped. He turned to see Alexis Sutherland. A woman of about fifty. A regular client of theirs. She had invited them to the party.

"When did you get here?" she said.

"Hi, Alexis," Maitland said. "A few minutes ago."

Alexis said, "Glad you could condescend to join us."

"She made me," Maitland said, nodding to Bianca.

"Right," Alexis said, smiling. She was aware of Maitland's attraction to Bianca. Unconsummated. Alexis could be a shit sometimes. Maitland still liked her.

Alexis leaned closer to him and said, "There's someone here that wants to talk to you."

"Who?" Maitland said.

"Max Glendenning."

Most people in the high-end antique business knew about Max Glendenning. He had a reputation for throwing people out of his Madison Avenue shop. He was one of the most sought out, successful antique dealers in New York. This in spite of the fact that no one much liked him. The man knew his trade.

Bianca said, "He's here?"

"Yes," Alexis said. "He's in the study." She lowered her voice. "We're not supposed to know."

Maitland said, "What's he want with me?"

17

"You'll have to ask him," Alexis said.

Alexis led Maitland up a grand staircase to a room on the second floor. She rapped on the door. A moment later, they heard the door being unlocked. Then it opened and there stood a man in his early seventies. He was a stout man, wearing a three-piece oxford suit and Buddy Holly glasses. "Yes?" he said, his tone imperious.

Alexis said, "Max, this is Evan Maitland. You wanted to speak to him?"

The man gave Maitland a sort of appraising look, not hiding it.

"Yes," he said. "Come in, will you?"

Maitland went in. Alexis seemed to hesitate and in that moment Max Glendenning closed the door in her face.

Maitland looked back to the door, smiled to himself. Locking doors and closing them on women's faces. The house didn't even belong to him.

The room was a study and it reeked of old money. Bookshelves to the ceilings, oak tables, two red leather chairs in front of a roaring fire. Between the chairs was a table with a bottle of port on it.

Glendenning motioned to the chairs. "Would you care for a drink, Mr. Maitland?" His accent was English, perhaps affected.

"No, thank you."

"Will you join me while I have one?"

"Sure."

They took seats in the red chairs. Glendenning took his glass and looked into the fire. He waited for a moment, comfortable with his silence. Maitland said nothing. Then Glendenning said, "Mr. Maitland, what do you know about me?"

"Not a lot," Maitland said. "You're a New York antique

dealer. You collect and sell English antiques. You're very good at it."

"What else?"

"I understand you can be a bit of a bully."

Glendenning turned and looked at Maitland. He was not intimidated, nor trying to intimidate.

Glendenning said, "I see you're a direct man. That's good. I am too."

"What can I do for you, Mr. Glendenning?"

"I'll come to that," Glendenning said. "First, I'd like to know a few things about you."

"Like what?"

"Is it true that you were a policeman?"

"Yes."

"In Chicago?"

"Yes."

"Is it true you were involved in criminal activities? That you were forced to resign?"

Maitland smiled. "Why do you want to know?"

"Because I don't like working with dishonest people. And I may want to offer you a job."

"I have a job."

"Yes, Colette's Antiques, is it?"

"Yeah."

"French wares?"

"French and Italian, mostly. But we try to suit all our clients' needs."

"And how is business this year?"

"It's okay."

"But not as good as last year?"

"Things are okay. Neither one of us is worried, if that's where you're going."

"No. I believe you misapprehend me. I'm not offering you a

full-time position. What I meant is, a temporary job."

"Doing what?"

"Finding an antique. An antique that's missing."

"I see," Maitland said. "Well, from what I understand, you're pretty good at doing that yourself."

"Most of the time," Glendenning said. "Tell me why you left the Chicago police."

Maitland shook his head. "I don't think that's any of your business."

The antiques dealer from New York looked at him. "Have you got something to hide?"

"No. But I don't believe in having to explain myself to people. My clients trust me. My partner trusts me. If you don't, you're free to move on and work with someone else."

"Yes, I suppose I am."

"Okay," Maitland said, standing.

"Just a minute," Glendenning said. "Sit down. Please."

Maitland stayed where he was. "Tell me what you've got in mind," he said.

"Mr. Maitland," Glendenning said, "I think I understand you better than you know. Working-class background, yes?"

Maitland said nothing. The man was right so far.

Glendenning said, "You tried to work for government, but it didn't work for you. You failed there and then made something of yourself in the antique business. A moderate success. But you miss the hunt, don't you? The excitement of the hunt. You don't really fit in this world, but you didn't fit in at the police department either."

Maitland looked at this man again. He was a sharp one, all right. Maitland asked, "What's it to you?"

"It's something I can see. I could see it even before I met with you. I've heard about you."

"Did you."

"What you did last year. To protect Ms. Garibaldi. You're a mercenary. A soldier of fortune."

"Are you patronizing me, Mr. Glendenning?"

"Not at all. I'm just making an observation. Besides, we're not so different, you and I. Do you know my background?"

"No."

"My mother and father were performers for the British Army. Sort of like the USO. My father was killed in one of the bombing raids. My mother had me and nothing else. So she married an American soldier and we moved to the States. My stepfather turned out to be a lout who left us as well and my mother had to raise me by herself. In a walk-up in Queens, no less. Those are my roots, Mr. Maitland. Working class, poor, humble. I built myself up from nothing. And, to be frank, an English accent helps in this business."

Maitland was surprised by this revelation. He said, "But you know antiques. No one has a better eye for English furniture than you."

"Oh, yes, I know my trade. But I also know my clients would rather believe I was to the manor born. I do not encourage this thinking, of course. But I don't discourage it either. As you know, antiques is a tough business. We have to use all we can."

"I do know."

"I tell you this not to gain your sympathy, Mr. Maitland. But to let you know I don't look down on you. Anymore than you look up to me."

After a moment, Maitland said, "Okay."

"We are both self-made. And, to a degree, we are both self-invented. I understand you hunt men, at times. Correct?"

"It's called bounty hunting. You're not hunting them like you would an animal; you're just bringing back someone who skipped out on bond. Anyway, it's something I used to do. But I stopped."

21

"When?"

"Last year."

"After that business with the Chinese gangsters?"

Maitland sighed. The man knew about it. "Yes," Maitland said. "That was part of it. But I told a friend I would stop."

"Ms. Garibaldi."

". . . yes."

Max Glendenning nodded. "She's a beautiful woman," Glendenning said.

"She's a friend," Maitland said, a little too quickly.

Glendenning raised a hand, signaling that it was not his intention to pry. He said, "Will you at least listen to my proposition?"

"Okay," Maitland said, and took a seat.

Glendenning said, "Have you heard of something called the Tarenton Hall chair?"

"I'm afraid I haven't."

"It's a carved mahogany open armchair bearing Tarenton arms. It was carved in the French rococo style of the 1750s. Its design is attributed to John Linnell."

"I think I am familiar with this," Maitland said. "Bianca is, anyway. It's a George II, correct?"

"Yes."

"It's my understanding you own that chair. That you refuse to sell it."

"I own *one* of the chairs, Mr. Maitland. It is one of a pair. The second one is in England. And I'd like to buy it."

"So buy it."

"I made arrangements to buy it. But last month it was stolen. I want you to find it for me."

"You want me to fly to London to find a chair?"

"Yes. I'll pay you well."

"But why? You already have one of the chairs."

"I want them both. It's not something I can explain to you."

"Do you have a buyer lined up for the pair?"

"No. You don't understand. I want them both for myself. For my own collection. I must have that chair."

"Did you say you bought it?"

"No. I said I made arrangements to buy it. I don't own it. But I want you to find it."

"It was stolen."

"Yes, perhaps."

"Did the London police perhaps investigate the theft?"

"I don't believe so."

Maitland regarded the man for a moment. "You don't believe so."

"They did not, Mr. Maitland."

"Well, I don't like the sound of this at all. Besides, I don't know anything about England. I've only been there once on a short vacation."

"You're good at finding things. You know antiques. And you can take care of yourself."

"You need someone based in England. Not someone like me."

"I need someone precisely like you. For reasons I've already given."

"What's the chair worth?"

"I've been offered a million for mine."

"Yeah, but what's it worth?"

"It's probably worth around $900,000. You bring it back to New York, I'll give you a ten percent finder's fee. That's $90,000."

"That's generous enough. But what if I come back with nothing?"

"I'll pay you twenty thousand dollars to make the trip. Plus expenses. Take ten days. If you don't find any leads, come back and keep the twenty thousand."

"What's to stop me from taking that money, going over there, watching television in my hotel room for ten days?"

"Absolutely nothing. But you won't collect your finder's fee. And you won't get to do what you like doing."

"What do you mean?"

"I mean you'd like to find that chair too. I can see it in your eyes. It would give you a certain legitimacy in this business."

"It might also give me a stretch in an English prison for trafficking in stolen goods."

"There's that chance, yes. If you're not careful. But you're generally careful, aren't you?"

"Yeah, generally. For instance, on something like this, I wouldn't go without having something in writing. And the twenty thousand up front."

"I'll draw up a contract in the morning."

"I haven't said yes yet."

"Sleep on it, then. I'll be leaving for New York tomorrow." Glendenning stood. "You know Gerry Willis, the hostess of this party?"

"I haven't met her yet."

"She just bought a center table from me. Mid-eighteenth century."

"What did she pay you?"

"Three hundred twenty." He paused, his sadness genuine. "I really hated to part with it. But sometimes you have to make room for new inventory."

Jesus, Maitland thought. Three hundred twenty thousand for a table. Maybe he should start using an English accent.

He found Bianca downstairs, a younger man flirting with her. She attracted younger men. She took Maitland's arm when he walked up.

The younger man noticed this, but kept on, saying, "Well, maybe I'll come by sometime."

Bianca smiled and said, "Sure." She did not introduce Maitland. The guy drifted away.

Maitland said, "I get the feeling I'm being used."

"You are," Bianca said.

Maitland said, "Handsome fella. You should be flattered. He doesn't look much older than thirty."

"A kick," Bianca said. "That's all he's looking for."

"No different than the rest of us," Maitland said. "Can we go? Or are there other young men you want to get to know here? I certainly don't want to cramp your style."

"Shut up," Bianca said and squeezed his arm. "One glass of wine. We'll take your car."

At a French bistro, she ordered a cup of soup with some bread and told the waiter she might have wine later. Maitland ordered a cup of coffee and watched her handle her meal. She had wonderful table manners.

Maitland told her about the meeting with Glendenning.

She said, "Well?"

"I told him I'd think about it," Maitland said. "Twenty thousand dollars is a lot of money. Another ninety if I bring back the chair. That's pretty good money."

"For you," Bianca said. "I'm left holding the store."

"I'd split it with you."

Bianca frowned. "Why would you do that?"

"It's not bounty hunting work," Maitland said. "It's antique work. We're partners, right?"

"I think so," Bianca said. "But you generally do what you want."

"Oh, is that so? You may recall, my dear, that I gave up something when you asked me to."

"There's that, yes," she said. "But I wonder if you're going back to it and not being honest about it."

Maitland said, "Glendenning wants me to find a chair, not a fugitive."

"And you miss the hunt," Bianca said. "Well, don't let me stop you."

"I won't," Maitland said, patting her hand.

THREE

It was about midnight Chicago time when the plane landed in London. It was the next morning in England. Maitland took a taxi from Heathrow to the Waring Hotel. After he checked into his room he undressed and climbed into bed and went straight to sleep. Six hours passed and when he awoke it was dark. He wondered how long it would take to adjust to the time change. He didn't like flying long distances. His last and only trip to London had been when he was married. He was still a policeman then. He had gotten homesick and he thought his wife was drinking too much at the pubs. At one point she'd said, "You could at least *try.*" The vacation had the unfortunate effect of placing them together for too long a time and may have inadvertently revealed to them that they weren't all that crazy about each other. Probably they had married too young and had grown apart. She left him about a year after they returned from the trip.

He had asked then, "Is there someone else?"

She had said, "What do you care?"

Twelve years passed and now he was in London again. This time he was working.

Maitland dressed in black slacks and a white shirt and a gray checked sport coat. With his coat over his arm, he took the small elevator down to the lobby. In the lobby he had coffee and a roll. The lobby and the tables were small and the servant was polite. Maitland studied a map of London while he had the coffee. He also looked at a small notebook.

Outside it was cold and damp and foggy. On the plane Maitland had looked out the window as the plane descended into a gray white mass. He waited for the clouds and fog to break before the plane reached the airport, but they never did.

Maitland pulled his scarf around his neck and tied up his raincoat. Then he walked to a bus stop and waited for a bus. Within ten minutes he saw the number he wanted and stepped on to a red double decker. He took a seat on the lower level.

Three miles away he stepped off and walked to a diamond store. He was surprised at how small the shop was. Not much bigger than the living room in his apartment. Behind the counter was a man in his sixties who reminded Maitland of Donald Pleasance in both look and manner. He wore an oxford suit with a vest, a checkered shirt and solid-colored tie. He was showing a set of diamond earrings to an Indian customer. Maitland heard him say, "She'll fancy that, sir." The Indian hesitated and the Englishman did not push him. Then the Indian nodded his head and soon they concluded the sale.

After the customer left, Maitland approached the counter. The Englishman looked at him and said, "Yes, sir?"

"Are you Jack Barrington?"

He regarded Maitland with a touch of wariness. "Yes," he said.

"I'm Evan Maitland. From Chicago. Harry Waters sends his regards."

Jack Barrington's expression relaxed. He extended his hand across the counter. Maitland shook it.

"Harry said you would be coming. How do you know him?"

"His son and I went to the police academy together."

"And you were mates?"

Maitland thought about that for a second. Then he realized the man was asking if they were good friends.

"We were friends," Maitland said, "yes. Harry said you were in the RAF together."

"Yes. In Korea."

"He also said you were in the military police."

"That's right."

"Perhaps you can help me then."

"Why? Are you in the military?"

"No. I'm in the antique business. I'm here to find a chair that may have been stolen."

The Englishman looked at him.

Maitland said, "It's a very expensive chair."

Barrington studied the American for a while. Then he said, "You don't know anyone in England, do you?"

"No, I don't."

Barrington sighed. Then he said, "There's a pub around the corner. St. George's. Give me a half hour and I can meet you there and we'll see what we can do."

The barmaid asked him what he wanted and he said a scotch and water. She left and returned with a glass filled to the quarter line with scotch. No ice. She set a small pitcher of water next to it.

"Anything else, dear?"

"No, ma'am," Maitland said, still looking at the small pitcher.

"Will you be having any supper?"

"Later, perhaps. What sort of sandwiches do you have?"

"We have ham and cheese." She didn't say anything else.

Finally, Maitland said, "Well, that sounds okay."

"Which?" the waitress said.

"Pardon?"

"Which would you like? The ham or the cheese?"

"Just a ham sandwich, I guess." She left and Maitland wondered why they didn't serve the ham with the cheese on top. Probably because it would taste good.

Jack Barrington arrived later and ordered a pint of bitters.

Maitland explained his position. The man he was representing, Max Glendenning, had been in negotiations with a fellow in Weybridge whose name was Alistair Lethbridge. Lethbridge claimed to have located the Tarenton chair and was willing to set up a purchase. But, two days before Glendenning was set to fly to London, Lethbridge called him and said the deal was off. Glendenning said, off? Why? Had Lethbridge found another buyer? No, Lethbridge said, the chair had been stolen. Then Lethbridge quickly ended the conversation.

Barrington said, "But your man still wants the chair?"

"Yes," Maitland said. "It means a lot to him. It's one of a pair and he owns the other."

"Why?"

"It could be because he wants to be able to sell the two as a pair," Maitland said. "But I doubt it. Glendenning is a collector. He likes having these things. It's his passion."

"And he's paying you for this mission?"

"Yes."

"Have you an interest in the chair as well?"

"No. I mean, normally, I would. But if I had it, I'd turn around and sell it. But this isn't a normal situation."

"You made an agreement with this man."

"Yes. I'm in the antique business too. It wouldn't do me any good to cheat Glendenning. And I wouldn't want to anyway."

"Have enough enemies already, do you?" There was a slight grin on Barrington's face.

"Enough," Maitland said.

Barrington said, "After the RAF, I thought about getting into the antiques business. But I decided against it. To begin with, it's an awful lot of work, having to hunt down these treasures. And it's rather competitive as well, isn't it?"

"Very."

"Yes. I'm glad I chose diamonds, jewelry," Barrington said. "Well, have you contacted the police?"

"No. Here's the problem: Lethbridge never identified the owner of the chair. So we don't know exactly if a theft was ever reported."

"Has it occurred to you that Lethbridge himself was lying? That there never was a chair?"

"It has. In fact, I asked Glendenning that. My thought was, Lethbridge was thinking about defrauding Glendenning, but then decided to back off. But Glendenning said Lethbridge knew too much about the chair, had been too detailed in his description."

"The chair itself was never authenticated?"

"No. I suspect Glendenning would have done that himself. Harry Waters said you might have friends at Scotland Yard."

"I do."

"Perhaps you could make a call."

"I can."

"Mr. Glendenning, of course, will pay for your time."

"Nonsense," Barrington said, lifting a hand. "Where are you staying?"

"The Waring Hotel. Near Victoria Station."

"Let me see what I can do," Barrington said. "I shall telephone tomorrow or the day after."

They shook hands and Barrington left. Maitland stayed and ate his ham sandwich alone.

FOUR

Later, Maitland walked to Piccadilly Circus, gave it a look, couldn't figure out what all the fuss was about, and walked back toward his hotel. He stopped at a pub. He had one pint of Guinness and then was told the pub would be closing in ten minutes.

He looked at his watch. Coming up on eleven o'clock. Four o'clock Chicago time. He was tired but not tired enough for bed. He had been told that there were nightclubs in London that were open later but he didn't know where they were and he didn't feel like asking anyone. Besides, he hated clubs, even at home.

He wondered what Bianca was doing. He could call her. But if he did he wouldn't know what to say. He felt guilty when he thought about her because he hadn't given her much of an explanation before he left. He *had* told her that he was going to England to look for a chair for Max Glendenning, but he hadn't told her much more than that. He hadn't told her that Glendenning had hinted that the job could be dangerous. Glendenning hadn't said that directly, but he had been honest enough to suggest it.

Besides, Bianca was in a bit of a strange place. She was separated from her husband. But she made a point of saying neither one of them had filed for divorce. It seemed she had not made up her mind. Maitland had found out recently that Bianca's husband was an alcoholic. Perhaps he was trying to clean himself up and Bianca didn't have the heart to divorce and abandon him if he was trying that. If he straightened out, would she leave him altogether? Or would she then see that he was worth going back to? It was hard to figure out. Maitland had never asked her. She was a private woman, not prone to discussing her marital problems. She was his partner and probably his closest friend. Though he didn't have many friends.

Maitland was generally comfortable by himself. But now he was away from home and he felt lonely. He didn't know London and London didn't know him.

He took a cab back to his hotel. The hotel bar was closed too and he took the elevator up to his room. He reviewed his notebook again and then tried to watch British television. He found some American shows: *Frasier* reruns and, for some reason, *Diagnosis: Murder.* He eventually left it on a rugby game between London and Leicester. He picked up a newspaper he'd bought in the lobby and looked at the headlines. Jennifer Aniston's latest break-up, Britney Spears's revelations, some pictures of good-looking British girls he'd never heard of. He thumbed through the paper for an hour and then read a Louis L'Amour paperback. Around two A.M. London time he managed to fall asleep.

The next morning he walked to a café for a late breakfast. He read the newspaper while he ate and then returned to his hotel. At the desk they gave him a message.

He made the telephone call from his hotel room.

Jack Barrington answered the phone. He said, "I spoke with an old colleague of mine at the Yard. To his knowledge, there were no reports of a theft of an antique you described. Not of that value."

"Okay," Maitland said.

"He did provide some information on Alistair Lethbridge.

Mr. Lethbridge is a dentist in Kensington. Rather successful, prominent one at that. However, I was advised that Lethbridge is, shall we say, an eccentric man."

Maitland said, "Can you explain that?"

"He is suspected to be on the wild side. Narcotics, sexual deviance, and so forth."

"Is he a drug dealer?"

"No, just a user, they believe."

"Any criminal activity at all?"

"No. However, the police have been around to his flat on reports of domestic disturbance. Apparently, Dr. Lethbridge likes men to rough him up."

"He's a homosexual."

"Yes, and more. Twice the neighbors have telephoned the police. Both times he refused to press charges against his assailants."

"Well, to each his own," Maitland said. "So he's never been arrested, but you were told he's a seedy character."

"I would say so, yes."

"Okay. Well, Mr. Barrington, I'm grateful to you."

"Think nothing of it. Mr. Maitland?"

"Yes?"

"If you're planning to see Dr. Lethbridge, I'd advise exercising caution. He may not be a dangerous man himself, but he prefers the company of dangerous men."

"I'll keep that in mind. Thanks again."

FIVE

The Austin taxi dropped Maitland off at a corner and he walked to a car rental agency. It was on a narrow lot in South London, canyoned by red brick businesses.

He found a Pakistani man in the small office near the front of the lot. The man was eating a Mars bar. On his desk was a small television.

"Yes?" the Pakistani said.

Maitland said, "I'd like to rent a car."

"Sorry. We are out of cars."

Maitland sighed. He pictured getting the phone book out again, taking another taxi to another part of the city. He said, "What about that red car out there? The one with the black vinyl top."

"The Ford?"

"Yes."

"That is not for hire. It belongs to my brother. He's trying to sell it."

"Can you rent—can you hire that out?"

"No. You can buy it, though. Twelve hundred pounds."

"Well, I don't want to buy it. I'm on vacation. Look, I'll pay for it. The same rate you charge to rent a new one."

"And insurance?"

"If I wreck it, I'll buy it."

"I will need fifty pounds, deposit."

"Fine. The car does work, does it?"

"Yes. In very good condition."

Maitland counted out the notes. He asked for a receipt. The man looked at him for a moment then gave him one. Then he opened a desk drawer and slid a key across.

There was no discussion of insurance or licensing. Maitland suspected there was probably something illegal being done, but the Pakistani wasn't going to say anything and Maitland wasn't going to ask.

Maitland walked out to the car. He saw that it was a Ford Granada Mark 1. A 1970s four-door sedan, nicely styled and fairly well preserved. Maitland had never seen one before. Manufactured in Europe, it looked nothing like the American Ford Granada, which Maitland had never liked.

The paint was a little faded on the trunk and hood and there was a trace of rust on the passenger's side wheel well, but the black vinyl top looked new and the interior was acceptable. It had a stick shift, which Maitland thought was unusual for a midsize sedan. But this was Europe.

Maitland opened the door and saw he was on the wrong side. He closed the passenger door and went around to the driver's side. Got in and started the car. The engine sounded healthy. With his left hand, he shifted the car into first gear and pulled it out into the road.

For a few blocks, he was uncertain. The roads were narrow and he would have to get used to driving on the other side. The interior of the car smelled faintly of tobacco. The six-cylinder engine pulled the car at a respectable speed. He would get used to it.

It took him about an hour to get to Weybridge. Greater London covered a lot of ground. He remembered reading somewhere that the entire population of the United States could be put in Texas and Texas still wouldn't be as densely populated as

England. Now he believed it.

Alistair Lethbridge lived in a townhouse on a narrow street. Maitland walked up to the front step and rang the doorbell. No one answered. He tried again. Still no answer. He walked back to the car. It was getting dark now. He didn't think about what time it was in Chicago. He walked away from the car and down the street. He was hungry.

He came to a tiny shop and went inside. He liked what he smelled. Greasy, but sort of comforting. In front of him a young boy gave his order, saying "Fish and chips, twice. Coca-Cola and orange drink."

Maitland took his place in line. When he got to the counter he ordered fish and chips and said, "to go." Then they knew he was an American. The staff was friendly to him, though not overly familiar. When they asked him what he'd like to drink, he asked for a bottled water, knowing it would cost him, but not wanting to risk tap water in another country, even England. The salesgirl flirted with him a little, saying, "Oh, he's sensible."

He took a seat at a small table near the front window.

The fish was very good. Better than any he'd tasted in the States. He didn't really know why. He wondered if it was something they did with the batter.

From the window, he looked at Alistair Lethbridge's house.

The shadows lengthened, the last of the gray daylight faded away. Maitland finished his meal and walked back to the Ford.

He waited in the car. The boredom came over him and he switched on the car radio. He listened to British voices discuss two football teams he'd never heard of. At times, he smiled. The people on the radio arguing in an English way, saying things like "You can have all that and bread."

It was almost seven P.M. when a shiny blue Rover pulled up to the townhouse. A thin man of about fifty got out of the driver's side. His skin was pale and he had wavy, swept-back hair. His clothes were tailored. Exiting the passenger side was a man no more than twenty-five. Not tall, but thick in the shoulders and legs. He reminded Maitland of the rugby players he had seen on television.

Maitland didn't like the look of him. He remembered what Barrington had told him. Alistair Lethbridge liked the rough boys, liked being knocked about, and this fella looked like he could do it with one hand.

Shit, Maitland thought. Why had he agreed to do this? A New York dealer approaches him and offers him money to track down an antique chair, knowing that there's danger involved and seeking Maitland out because of it. Seeing Maitland's weakness.

In the States, Maitland would have been prepared to take on a bigger, stronger adversary. The thing to do was to come prepared, armed with weapons and be ready to fight dirty. In the States, he would have had a gun or, at a minimum, pepper spray or a taser. But you couldn't bring guns into England.

Maitland looked at his watch. Let fifteen minutes pass. Then he got out of the car and walked up to the front door of the townhouse.

He rang the bell again and Lethbridge came to the door.

He was in shirt sleeves and club tie. He was also wearing an apron, a black chef's sort.

"Yes?"

"Mr. Lethbridge?"

"Yes."

"My name is Maitland. I'm an antiques dealer from Chicago. May I speak to you?"

"What about?"

"I have a piece of furniture I'm trying to sell. A Chippendale table. I wondered if you'd be able to help me."

Lethbridge's expression lightened. "I see," he said. "You are looking for a buyer?"

"Yes. I can't—" Maitland looked around, as if he were concerned someone might be watching. "I can't take it back to the States. I have to unload it here, in London."

"Perhaps I can help you. For a reasonable fee, of course."

"Of course."

"Come in then."

The interior of the townhouse was modern. High ceilings, white chairs and carpet, a table made of solid marble. A grand piano took up much of the front room.

Lethbridge said, "I was cooking. Do you mind if we speak in the kitchen?"

"Not at all."

Maitland followed him through a narrow hall to the kitchen area. In the kitchen was another marble stand. On the stand was a blue and white ceramic bowl. Next to that a carton of eggs. Lethbridge spoke as he broke the eggs over the ceramic bowl. This he did with one hand.

"Do you cook, Mr. Maitland?"

"A few things."

"I find it very relaxing. My friend and I were going to have a quick supper before we went out to the clubs."

The young man came out of the bedroom. He wore tight European designer jeans and an Izod shirt. He eyed Maitland with hostility.

"Who's this?"

"This is Mr. Maitland, Eric. He's only going to be here for a moment."

Maitland looked at the younger man. Gay, but no effeminacy to him. Maitland gave him a friendly, nonthreatening smile, but not much more. He said, "How are you doing?"

Eric looked at Maitland in an unusual way and said to Lethbridge, "Him too?"

Maitland didn't like the sound of that.

And Lethbridge looked over at Maitland, appraising him for a moment. Then Lethbridge said, "I don't believe so, Eric. He's not of our school, I suspect."

Eric looked at Maitland and pointed at the front door and said, "Piss off, then."

"Excuse me?" Maitland said.

"Out," Eric said. "Before I knock your fucking teeth out."

"Now, Eric," Lethbridge said. A plea perhaps, but Maitland could see that Lethbridge was getting a charge out of this too.

Maitland looked at Eric. Younger, tougher, and probably a lot meaner. Maitland asked, "You want to fight me?"

Eric looked back at him and laughed. "Won't be much of a fight, you fucking ponce."

"Okay," Maitland said. "Let's step outside."

"Eric—" Lethbridge said, his tone irritated but not scared. As if to say, *not now.*

"Excuse me," Maitland said to Lethbridge. Then he crooked a finger at Eric and said, "Let's go."

Eric followed him and Maitland kept far enough ahead of him to prevent from being hit in the back of the head. Maitland reached the front door and opened it. Stepped out to the cold night and stopped. Eric reached the doorway, crossed through it and Maitland grabbed his shirtfront with both hands and pulled him hard and quick, turning and twisting him as he did so.

The bigger man stumbled forward, not expecting it. Eric went down the front steps, still stumbling, not falling but struggling to keep his feet. He went to one knee but got back up, quickly, ready to turn around and plunge his fist into the American's face.

But when he turned around all he saw was the front door

slamming shut. Then he heard the door being locked from the inside.

In the house, Maitland locked all the locks he could find. Then he looked through the window to see Eric charging back up the steps. Maitland heard the man striking his fists against the locked door as he walked quickly to the kitchen.

He walked past a confused Lethbridge to the back door and made sure that was locked too.

Maitland returned to Lethbridge.

Lethbridge said, "Where's Eric?"

Maitland said, "He decided to get some air. Cool off."

They both heard the sounds of the front door being pounded with fists. Eric demanding to be let in, using some choice words.

Now Lethbridge was looking at Maitland in a different way. "Where did you say you were from?"

"Chicago. And I lied to you earlier. I'm not trying to sell a stolen antique. I'm looking for one."

"Who are you?"

"My name is Maitland. I'm here on behalf of Max Glendenning."

Alistair Lethbridge looked over at him, the realization dawning.

"Yeah," Maitland said.

"I see," Lethbridge said. He began whisking the eggs in the bowl. "Well, as I told Mr. Glendenning, I'm no longer in a position to negotiate the sale of the Tarenton Hall chair. Are you a policeman?"

"No," Maitland said. "Why aren't you in a position?"

"A gentleman contacted me and said he would like to sell it. Through my contacts, I knew of Mr. Glendenning's interest. However, when the time came close, the gentleman said he no longer wanted to sell it."

"Did he say why?"

"He did not."

"Did he sell it to someone else?"

"I was not told."

"Can you find out?"

"Why should I, Mr. Maitland?"

"Mr. Glendenning wants to buy the chair. I'm sure he'd be willing to pay for information about it."

"How much?"

"A thousand pounds. If the information was helpful. And if the provenance showed the chair to be authentic."

"That's two contingencies, Mr. Maitland. And considerable ones at that. I prefer cash up front."

"I'll tell you what," Maitland said. "I'll give you five hundred pounds for the name of the man who owns the chair."

"Five hundred pounds." Lethbridge gestured to the high-dollar kitchen around him. "Do I look like a man in need of funds?"

Maitland said, "The best of us can get overextended once in a while. Plus, it would be tax free."

Lethbridge laughed. Then he gave Maitland a steady look and said, "I suppose you think I'm a fraud, don't you?"

"I think you're a man who likes to operate in the shadows." Maitland smiled. "No harm in that, so long as we can do business together."

"Give me a day to think about your proposition. Where can I reach you?"

"I'm staying at the Waring Hotel."

"Ah, one of London's finest. Mr. Glendenning's compliments, I suppose."

It was a snobbish jab, of the English sort. Maitland almost appreciated it. He'd never had any real illusions about his station in life.

A rapping now, coming from the back door.

Lethbridge sighed. "That would be Eric. Would you be a dear and let him in?"

"No," Maitland said, "I don't think I will. Give it some thought, Mr. Lethbridge."

Maitland walked to the front of the house and let himself out. He was driving away when Eric charged out the front door, shouting things at him.

SIX

Maitland put the Ford in an underground car park. Then he walked to his hotel. It was a long walk. He hadn't thought about the problems of having a car in London. But it was okay. He wouldn't be here long.

In the hotel room he locked the door and put a chair against it. He did not try to force himself to sleep. He watched television until three and then he shut his eyes.

He woke about four hours later. Faint light coming into the room. He showered and shaved and dressed. He packed his bags and walked to the underground garage. Then he drove south, out of the center of the city.

The roads were twisty and narrow. It seemed different, away from the Piccadilly Circus and Big Ben. It was plain and gray and brown and probably unappealing to tourists. Maitland liked it.

He liked the '76 Ford Granada too. But it didn't have a GPS. He circled a park twice, not planning to, then he stopped and asked for directions. Ten minutes after that he found the bed and breakfast.

It was a slice of a building set between other slices. Gray with white shutters on the windows. There was no sign and no evidence that it was open to the public. Maitland rang the bell and a heavyset woman came to the door. She was shabbily dressed and she held a cigarette. Maitland wondered if he had the right address.

"Yes?"

"Do you rent rooms?"

"Yes."

"Oh, good. I didn't see a sign."

"Sign's being repaired. Expect to have it ready by March." She took a drag on her cigarette, then folded her arms. "Not exactly the height of tourist season, is it?"

"No. What I meant was, do you have a room available now?"

"We've got one room available. Thirty pounds, breakfast included. No telly in the room, though."

"That's alright. I don't need one. Would I be your only guest?"

"You would."

"How about you don't make me breakfast, then? I'd still pay the same rate."

"Breakfast's included, dear."

Maitland pictured himself sitting alone at a breakfast table with this woman. He said, "Really, it's not necessary."

"Right then. Like to see the room, 'fore you commit yourself?"

"Sure."

He followed her up a narrow staircase. She showed him to a room at the front of the house. The bed was no wider than a cot. But it looked clean and well kept.

The woman said, "Like to see the loo?"

"Sure."

That was clean too and Maitland said it would be fine.

The woman said, "I'm Mrs. Cavendish. There's coffee and tea if you like in the kitchen. And biscuits. And I do ask for two days' payment in advance."

Maitland gave her the money. Then followed her downstairs.

He said, "If I park in the street, will I get ticketed?"

"Sorry?"

"Is it legal to park on the street? Do I need some sort of permit?"

"Not out here, love. There's a garage in the back, room for two cars. You can park your car in there if you like."

"I may take you up on that. Is there a telephone I can use?"

"Yes. In the kitchen. Not calling long-distance, are you?"

"No. In fact, I'll be buying a cell phone this afternoon."

She smiled. "Right," she said. "Well, I'll leave you to it."

She went into the living room where she had left the television on.

Maitland called the Waring Hotel and asked the desk clerk if he had any messages.

"Yes," the desk clerk said.

Maitland waited for the clerk to connect him to a recorded message, but then listened as the clerk read him two numbers, the way a law office receptionist would. A Mr. Barrington and a Mr. Lethbridge. Maitland wrote the numbers down.

Maitland went up to the room and unpacked. He left the house and drove to a nearby Boots where he bought some disposable razors, soap and shampoo. He paid for the items, shaking his head at the prices. He asked the sales clerk where he could buy a temporary cell phone. The sales clerk directed him to the British equivalent of Best Buy, which was further south. Maitland bought the phone there.

From the privacy of his car, he called Barrington first.

Barrington said, "Did you contact Lethbridge?"

"I did," Maitland said. "I made him an offer. He said he's going to think about it."

"Are you aware he has an office in Kensington?"

"I am. I have the number."

"There's something else," Barrington said. "A friend of my daughter's used to work at Sotheby's. I thought she might know something about the Tarenton chair. Would you like her telephone number?"

"Did you already speak to her about this?"

"No."

"Okay," Maitland thought for a moment. He felt a bit uneasy about telling too many people his business in London.

"No," Barrington said again. "I'll leave that to you. But she might be of some help."

"Okay. Yeah, maybe I will talk to her."

"Her name is Sophie Palmer." Barrington gave him the number.

Maitland said, "Have you given her the heads-up I might be calling?"

". . . sorry?"

Maitland said, "Have you forewarned Miss Palmer I might be calling?"

"Yes. She has been advised."

"Okay. Thanks for your assistance."

"You're welcome."

Maitland hung up the phone. He wondered if he had ever thanked anyone for their assistance before. These people could get you talking like them.

Next he called Lethbridge.

Lethbridge answered the phone, which sounded more like a cell phone than an office phone. *Good,* Maitland thought. *Better to have his cell phone.*

Maitland said, "This is Evan Maitland. You called?"

"Ah, yes."

"Well," Maitland said, "are you willing to give me the owner's name?"

"Possibly . . ."

"What do you mean, possibly? You are or you aren't."

"I think we should discuss it again. Perhaps we can come to terms."

"Alistair, you're getting kinda squirrelly on me."

"Squirrelly? What a funny phrase. Here we would say apprehensive."

"Try evasive. You say we should meet again. Why? So you can have your boy exact his vengeance?"

"There shall be none of that. Meet me at the Blue Hat Club tonight at nine o'clock. We can discuss your chair then."

". . . I don't know."

"But I do, Mr. Maitland. That's why you'll be there at nine o'clock sharp. Or you can return to the States with nothing. Ta."

Maitland heard a dial tone. "Shit," he said. Punked by a guy who ended conversations with *ta*.

SEVEN

The American agent extended his hand to the two detectives from Scotland Yard and said, "Joe Roddy, United States Treasury."

The American agent wore a blue pin-stripe suit with a pressed white shirt and a red tie. An American flag was pinned to his lapel. His hair was slicked back with some sort of pomade and there was the faint smell of skin conditioner about him. Had the Englishmen been aware of the American NBA, they would have suspected that Joe Roddy modeled himself after Pat Riley.

The Scotland Yard policemen were Detective Inspector (DI) Ronald Martin and Detective Sergeant (DS) Bill Raines. Inspector Martin was a tall, sallow, rat-faced sort of man with an unpleasant smile. Sergeant Raines was a big man, six-three, with broad shoulders and a barrel chest and a thick, shaggy mustache. Both of them were taller than Joe Roddy.

Joe Roddy sized the detectives up. Roddy put much stock in people's appearances and he thought these guys looked a little rough. Unkempt and unprofessional. Bordering on shabby. It was his first time meeting men of the Yard. He had expected the detectives to look like Oxford professors. He told himself if Raines were under his command, he'd order him to shave the mustache, pronto. He would tell them they couldn't look like slobs and work in his unit.

Joe Roddy had an MBA from George Mason and a law degree from the University of Michigan. He was the son of two teachers, neither one of whom he had ever much liked or respected. At the same time he resented and distrusted those who had succeeded in the private sector. He believed he had found a home in federal law enforcement. He was shorter than average, but handsome, with a build similar to a gymnast's, and he had good teeth. He was vain, even by a cop's standards, and he was ambitious. He had started at Treasury in Los Angeles, moved to Washington and then was assigned to Chicago.

He had sought this assignment because he believed it was high profile.

He exchanged pleasantries with the men of Scotland Yard, making small talk that they responded to uncomfortably. He made mild jokes about his flight to London and the weather and received polite, thin smiles in response.

Then Joe Roddy removed his smile and said, "Okay, let's get down to business." His hands now on his waist, arms akimbo. The authoritative look. Coach Riley addressing Kareem and Magic.

Roddy said, "The man we're looking for is Vincent DeGiusti. We believe he's in possession of eight million dollars' worth of bearer bonds stolen in Naperville, Illinois, approximately three weeks ago. We believe DeGiusti is coming to London to sell those bonds through, or to, the Shivers brothers. And you know who they are."

The Scotland Yard detectives said nothing.

Joe Roddy took a breath and said, "The goal, gentlemen, is to catch Mr. DeGiusti with those bonds. I'll bring him back to Chicago where he and his friends will face criminal charges. What you do with the Shivers is your business."

Sergeant Raines did not smile. He said, "How are you so sure your man's coming to London? Why not try to unload them in Switzerland or Rio de Janeiro?"

"Because it'll be easier here. Or, I should say, they need to go through here. To sell those bonds, they'll need forged certificates. They don't have anyone on their team capable of doing that. The Shivers do have someone."

"You mean a fixer?" Inspector Martin said.

"Yes. A fixer. Forger, whatever term you guys use."

Martin said to the American, "Do you know who this fixer is?"

"No. But I'm counting on you guys to help us out there. We know the fixer, we can get DeGiusti cold."

The Englishmen exchanged glances.

Martin asked, "Where is DeGiusti now?"

"We don't know."

"You mean," Martin said, "you don't know if he's in England?"

"We haven't confirmed a sighting, no. But we expect him here."

Martin said, "You mind me asking why?"

"The Salvetti's lawyer flew here last week. His name is Lewis Dushane. We believe he was doing advance work, setting things up with the Shivers."

"I see," Inspector Martin said. "And you have evidence he rendezvoused with the Shivers?"

"No. Not hard evidence. But we have good reason to believe he did."

Sergeant Raines gave him a steady look and said, "Good reason."

Joe Roddy flushed and said, "Look, you guys want to be difficult, I can go to your DCI. You're supposed to cooperate with me."

"No need for that, guv'nor," Martin said, smiling a little at the little man losing his cool. "We'll assist you. If we seem to be lacking the enthusiasm you'd prefer, you have to understand something about the Shivers brothers."

"What's that?" Roddy said.

"That they're not easily nicked," Sergeant Raines said.

"Excuse me?" Roddy said.

Inspector Martin said, "What the sergeant is saying is that the Yard has stacks upon stacks of investigative material and criminal charges on Ian and Ken Shivers, but they have neither one of them ever been incarcerated. They have contacts, a network into some blokes higher than us. It's all a bit murky. Criminal charges get dismissed, evidence gets lost, witnesses clam up or altogether disappear."

Raines said, "We can't get anyone to testify against them."

"What's more," Martin said, "they're bloody celebrities. Charmers. Go to their club you'll see half of last week's Page Three girls, dancing about, flashing their udders. Funny blokes too. Have a pint with Kenny, and odds are he'll have you laughing yourself silly. He's a regular joker. After that, he'd as like cut your eye out with a bread knife. 'Course, Ian's a cold-eyed killer too, but he's mostly rational. When he strikes, he's got a reason, usually. For Ian, it's mostly business. But Ken. Kenny's a fucking volcano. You don't know when he'll erupt. In the last five years, while Her Majesty's government has concentrated on Pakis and Muslim bomb throwers, these two have basically taken over South London. Gambling, pornography, long firm fraud, extortion and loan sharking. The point is, Mr. Roddy, we've been trying to bring these two down for a long time and it's no easy task. So pardon us if we seem a bit skeptical when a man like you, an American agent, drops into London and suggests that we've got an open and shut case."

"I wasn't suggesting that," Roddy said.

" 'Course not," the inspector said, though they both knew he was. Inspector Martin made a friendly gesture. "But we'll work with you."

Joe Roddy nodded. He gave Sergeant Raines a look, then he

walked to the door and let himself out.

When he was gone, Raines said, "Wanker."

Inspector Martin smiled and said, "He's an up and comer. Who's fixing for the Shivers these days?"

Sergeant Raines said, "What about Mario Lestor?"

"Naw," Martin said. "Not on something like this. This is out of Mario's element. I'd say it was Julian Atherton. I've no doubt of it, actually."

EIGHT

There was a Rolls Royce and a vintage Mercedes 600 limousine in front of the Blue Hat Club and the sight of them made Maitland nervous. He was on an expense account, but three hundred dollar meals weren't something he felt comfortable with. He would order a drink or a cup of coffee, conduct his business with Lethbridge, and get out.

The layout was unusual. There were tables in a rather small front room and a bar, but there weren't many people seated at the tables and the ones who were seemed unhappy and restless. There was also a small bar with one bartender behind it. But the place was noisy and soon Maitland realized that this was only a part of the club. The part they made people sit at who weren't welcome. There was a buzz of conversation and music coming from another room behind a door with a red curtain. Next to that doorway stood a large man wearing a dark blue suit. The man was chewing gum. Sitting on the stool next to the man was a girl of about twenty wearing a black leather mini-skirt and a gold lamé top plunging halfway down her front. Cheap jewelry around her neck and on her wrists.

Maitland approached them.

The man gave him a sort of up and down look. The girl ignored him. The man said, "Yeah."

"I'm supposed to meet someone here."

"Who?"

"Alistair Lethbridge."

"What's your name?"

"Maitland."

The man gave his gum a couple more chews, than gestured to the girl. She came down off her stool and vanished behind the curtain. Maitland and the blue suit bouncer continued not to acknowledge each other.

The girl returned and nodded to the bouncer. He said, "Okay," and Maitland followed the girl through the curtain.

It was bigger behind the curtain. Alive and crowded. The patrons having fun, drinking and socializing. A haze of smoke and the smell of gin and wine and steaks and fries. The lighting was low, the tables topped with white tablecloths, the chairs backed with red leather. There were other young women dressed like the one who was leading Maitland. Flash and sparkly, brassy and bold. Cheap-looking, one might say. But the clothes were designer and actually very expensive. Some of them were wives or girlfriends of British football players, and they were often featured in the pages of one of London's many daily news-papers. Some of the football player husbands were there too, dressed in warm-up suits and wearing gold chains. Multimil-lionaires dressing tacky because they liked it.

Mixed with that were people who looked like they worked in Britain's financial district. Tailored suits, most of them dark blue or gray. Not many of them accompanied by women.

Alistair Lethbridge wore a gray suit with a checked shirt and silk tie. With him was another man in a shiny black suit, white shirt with cufflinks, no tie. Lethbridge gestured for Maitland to take a seat and the girl left them alone.

"Maitland, this is Julian. Julian, Maitland."

Maitland shook hands with Julian Atherton.

Julian Atherton was a thin man of about forty with a well-trimmed beard. He wore spectacles and his hair was cut close to the scalp and over his forehead in the British fashion.

Maitland thought about asking Lethbridge if his friend Eric would be joining them, but decided against it. He needed Lethbridge's help, and there was no need to embarrass him. Presuming he could be embarrassed. He wondered if Julian was the hurtin' kind too.

Julian said, "Will you have a drink, Mr. Maitland?"

"Yes. A Scotch."

Using two fingers Julian signaled a waitress over and gave her the order. He added a gin and tonic for Lethbridge.

Maitland looked about the room again. On the other side of the room a man sat at a table with a beautiful woman. The man wore jeans and a T-shirt and no shoes or socks. At the man's feet was a German Shepherd.

Lethbridge said, "Recognize that chap?"

"No," Maitland said.

"That's Jeffrey Holt, the Formula 1 champion. Eccentric, isn't he?"

"Yeah. They let him bring a German Shepherd in here?"

"We don't call them German Shepherds in Britain, Maitland. We call them Alsatians. What with the war and all."

"Hasn't enough time passed?"

"Not for us."

The waitress returned with the drinks. Maitland sipped his and guessed it was Glenlivet.

Julian said, "Alistair says you're interested in a Tarenton chair."

"I am," Maitland said. "Are you the owner?"

"No."

Silence at the table. Maitland looking from one man to the other.

Maitland said, "Then what?"

"I know the owner."

"Who is it?"

"He prefers to remain anonymous."

"Why?"

"He just does."

"Well, I'm sorry, but that's not going to work."

Julian Atherton said, "Why not?"

"Because my client only buys his items in good faith. He's not interested in buying stolen goods."

Another silence.

Lethbridge said, "Are you suggesting we're thieves, Mr. Maitland?"

"Not at all. But we are talking about a very expensive antique here. So we have to be cautious."

Julian Atherton smiled at the American diplomacy. "As do we," Julian said.

Maitland said, "If we can come to terms, we'd certainly be willing to agree to keep the seller's name secret. If that's what he wants."

Julian said, "How much are you willing to pay?"

"Hard to say without seeing it and authenticating it. But if the chair is in good condition, perhaps as much as $800,000."

"Hmmm," Julian said. "Maybe more."

"Maybe," Maitland said.

The tone of the crowd changed. A couple of men had come in and the patrons paid attention. Maitland looked at them and at first thought they were twins. Then saw that one of them was heavier than the other. They were brothers. Well dressed and swaggering. Maitland felt the hair go up on his neck. There was something fearsome about these two. He had seen into the eyes of a few killers in his time and he recognized the look. Now the heavy one went over to the Formula 1 champion's table. The Formula 1 champ greeted him with a big smile and a handshake. Maitland could see that the Formula 1 champ wasn't scared of the man, but then he was probably too stupid to be scared.

Maitland knew fear could be a gift and he respected it.

Now the other brother—the thin one—was coming over to their table.

Ian Shivers put a hand on Julian Atherton's shoulder.

"Hello, Julian."

"Hello, Ian."

"Enjoying the meal?" Ian said.

"We did. I had the roast chicken."

Ian said, "You should try our bacon butties. As good as your mum's." Ian Shivers looked at Lethbridge and said, "Alistair."

"Hello, Ian," Lethbridge said. And Maitland could see that Lethbridge was frightened of the man.

Then Ian Shivers looked at Maitland. A direct look that unnerved him. Though Maitland knew how to hide his fear. Sometimes.

Ian said, "And who might you be?"

"Evan Maitland."

"From the States, are you?"

"Yes. Chicago."

Ian looked at him for a few moments. A look of apprehension there, brief, then it was gone. He said, "On holiday, are you?"

"Sort of."

Ian Shivers smiled at the evasion. "Right," Ian said. Still smiling, he said, "Well, as you long as you behave yourself."

He maintained the stare just long enough to let Maitland know he was being threatened. Maitland looked back at him, not smiling or frowning or showing much of anything. Ian Shivers walked off.

"Friendly fellow," Maitland said.

"This is his club," Lethbridge said. "His and his brother's. They—"

"Alistair," Julian said, his voice sharp.

Lethbridge looked up at Julian. He took the warning and dropped it.

Maitland looked from Julian to Lethbridge and then back to Julian again.

Julian said, "Maybe we can do a deal. Let me speak to the owner tomorrow. May I call you?"

"Yeah." Maitland took out a pen and his small pad and wrote a number on the sheet and tore it off. "Here's my cell number."

"Alistair says you're staying at Waring," Julian said.

"Yes. But I'm usually out during the day."

"Of course."

"I'll say good night then," Maitland said. He stood and left.

He was relieved when he got outside. The Shivers brothers had frightened him and he was not ashamed of it. There are times a man walks into a bar or maybe even just a room and he feels the hairs on the back of his neck stand up and he knows it's trouble. If you're a police officer on duty or a bounty hunter seeking a jumper, leaving may not be an option. But if you're just a man, usually the best thing to do is turn around and walk out. Too much glass in a bar, as a wise man once said. Though he suspected both the Shivers were familiar with many weapons beyond glass.

NINE

"Ms. Palmer?"

"Yes?"

"My name is Maitland. Jack Barrington gave me your number."

"Oh. I see. How are you?"

"I'm fine. I just left a club in central London. I wondered if I could meet with you to discuss an antique."

"This evening?"

"If possible, yes."

"It's possible, yes. Do you know where the Ritz is?" Sophie Palmer's voice was soft but direct.

Maitland said, "I think so."

"Well, you do or you don't."

Maitland smiled. "I have maps," he said.

"Right. Can you meet me there in an hour?"

"That would be great."

Sophie Palmer said, "You're an American, of course. But I shan't know what you look like."

"I'll be wearing shorts and a ball cap."

Silence.

"Sorry?"

"I was joking . . . about . . . tourists. I'm in a raincoat and brown suit."

"Oh, I see, a joke." Another uncomfortable silence. She said, "Well, I'll be wearing a raincoat too. Tan mackintosh. Oh, and

Mr. Maitland?"

"Yes."

"We don't say 'Ms.' in Britain. It's Mrs. or Miss."

"Okay," Maitland said. He wouldn't ask her which she was.

He was in the lobby of the Ritz, looking around and still feeling stupid about the ball cap and shorts joke. Then a woman signaled him and he walked over.

She was seated at a table. A blond woman, fair complexion, in her mid-thirties. Her tan raincoat was open, showing a black skirt and powder blue blouse beneath.

She said, "Are you Mr. Maitland?"

"Yes. Sophie?"

"Yes. Sit down, please."

Sophie Palmer did not open her mouth to smile, but her eyes had some warmth and her body was relaxed. She said, "Would you like a drink?"

"Well . . . I had one earlier."

"Only one?"

"Well, I don't drink much."

"You Americans. You drink too much or not at all. No middle ground." Now she smiled.

"I guess I can have another."

She called a waiter over. The waiter wore a white servant's jacket and black pants. Sophie ordered another vodka tonic and Maitland ordered a Scotch and water. The waiter left.

Sophie said, "Your first time in London?"

"No. I was here before, over ten years ago. Actually, it was about fifteen years ago. It seems cleaner now."

"Was it dirty before?"

Maitland smiled uncomfortably. "No. It just seems cleaner now."

She smiled back, letting him know she was teasing him. She

said, "It is cleaner, I suppose. A lot of money has come into London in the last ten years. When I finished university, you could rent a flat in central London for not much money. Now it's strictly for the very rich. Now it's an international city."

"Wasn't it always?"

"It was and it wasn't. I suppose it's difficult to explain."

The waiter returned with their drinks.

He left and Sophie said, "How do you know Mr. Barrington?"

"He was in the RAF with a friend of mine's father. The friend and I went to the academy together."

"The academy . . . military?" She pronounced it "militry."

"No. Police academy."

"You're a policeman?"

"I used to be. I work in antiques now."

"How does that happen? A policeman comes to be in the antique business."

"It's a long story."

There was silence between them. Maitland glancing at her, but not so long as to be rude. She was very pretty.

She said, "That's it, then?"

"Pardon?"

"It's a long story, but you're not going to tell me what it is."

"No. It would bore you."

"You know, you're not typical, are you?"

"What do you mean?"

"I mean, most Americans tell you their life story within five minutes of meeting you. We're not like that."

"We . . . you mean Britons?"

"Yes."

"Well, not all Americans are like you think."

"Oh, I see. You know what I think."

"You've told me what you think."

"I've made a generalization. Is that it?"

"Sort of."

She said, "Would you mind if I had a cigarette?"

"No."

She removed a pack of Dunhills from her purse and lit her own cigarette. She was a smooth smoker, not jittery. Maitland decided she was not irritated with him.

She said, "You know, my brother wanted to be a policeman. He had been in the SAS and he had applied to the London Metropolitan Police."

"Did they take him?"

"Yes. They took him. But . . . well, he was killed before training begun. Motor accident."

"I'm sorry."

"It's alright. I'm sorry."

"You're sorry . . . for what?"

"For burdening you with that," she said. She looked at him and said, "You're looking for an antique?"

"Yes." Maitland waited. He figured out she wasn't going to discuss her brother's death anymore. She was genuinely sorry for bringing it up and it would offend her if he didn't let her change the subject.

She asked, "What is it?"

"It's a Tarenton chair." He explained where it had come from and who he was working for. He did not tell her about Glendenning's humble roots. He did tell her about meeting with Alistair Lethbridge and Julian Atherton.

Sophie said, "They won't tell you who the owner is?"

"No."

"Do you suspect a fraud?"

"It's possible. To be frank, these guys seem a little seedy."

"You don't trust them."

"No."

"Well, that's good. Has it occurred to you that the owner

may be of the aristocracy?"

"Living in a castle but having trouble paying for the taxes? That sort of thing?"

"Simplistic, but yes. That sort of thing."

"Yes, it's occurred to me. That's why I told them I would keep the seller's identity confidential if they wanted."

"And would you?"

"Would I what?"

"Would you maintain the confidence?"

"I would. And my client would too." Maitland said, "Mr. Glendenning is not a vain or vulgar man. Not in the way you might think. He would take no pleasure in telling people he bought a chair from a cash-poor baron or earl. He's not like that. I don't think he is, anyway. He's a collector. These things have value to him, beyond money, beyond prestige. Can you understand that?"

"Of course. But he already has one, doesn't he?"

"He wants the other too. Would it be such a blow to England if he were to purchase it?"

"It's of no consequence to me." She paused then said, "I'm sorry, what is your first name?"

"Evan."

"Evan Maitland. That's a Scottish name, you know."

"Maitland?"

"Yes. My people are Scottish as well. My grandfather came to London before the war. Do you know when yours came to the States?"

"It was my great-grandfather. He came to Chicago after the First World War. Married a French-Canadian girl . . ."

"Are your mum and dad alive?"

"No."

"Any brothers, sisters?"

"No."

"Family of your own?"

"No. I was married before . . . we had planned on having children, but . . . well. She's married to someone else now. Had a kid with him." He added, "He's a good kid."

Sophie looked at him and said, "No regrets, then?"

"No. I guess I don't think about it much."

"How British." She smiled again. "Most of us live the lives we choose."

"Maybe," he said. "Do you have children?"

"Yes. A little boy. He's on holiday with his dad in Switzerland."

"Oh."

"We're divorced."

"Oh."

She made a gesture that perhaps meant he shouldn't read too much into it. Or maybe it meant he shouldn't push her too hard or too soon. He liked her though.

Maitland said, "You think you can help me?"

Sophie said, "Maybe. I don't work in antiques anymore. But I can check around and see if I can discover the owner. If I do, perhaps you'll be able to contact him directly. Or perhaps I can contact him for you. In a discreet way."

"I would be okay with that," Maitland said.

"We'll see. I have your telephone number."

"It's good as long as I'm in London." He handed her a business card. "That's my number in Chicago. In case you're ever there."

TEN

Julian Atherton parked his Aston Martin on the street known as Savile Row and walked into one of the shops.

Inside an extremely thin man in a silk shirt stood behind a counter. He was showing shirts to a customer. He lifted his head to Julian when he walked in.

"Morning, Julian."

"Morning, Brian."

Brian said, "He's in the back."

Julian walked through the store to a private dressing room. In the room, Harold, the black beauty, stood on a small pedestal as an elderly tailor measured his arm. Kenny Shivers was saying, "It's gotta have the proper drape, Adrian."

And young Harold was saying, "But I'd like something more pastel—"

And then Ken was saying, "Shut up, you ponce."

Julian Atherton kept his smile to himself. Harold would get some nice clothes, a couple of new suits, and a few bruises and in three weeks Ken would find himself another chicken. He seemed to prefer the darker-haired ones, the black princes. Ken Shivers freely used terms like ponce and poof and queer but everyone knew never to apply such terms to him. He could say it, but no one else could. Not around him and certainly never about him. A man from the East End had once called Ken a "fat poof" and Ken had pushed him off his bar stool and plunged a knife into his throat.

Now Ken said, "Hello, Julian."

"Morning, Ken. You wanted to chat?"

"Yes. Ian said there was an American with you at the club last night."

"Yes."

"Who was he?"

"His name was Maitland."

"What's he about, then?"

"In town on business."

"What sort of business, Julian?"

"Er, furniture. He's an antiques dealer. A friend of Alistair's, really. I only met him briefly."

"Ian said he's from Chicago."

"Yes, I believe he is."

"Well, that's a bit of a fucking problem, wouldn't you say?"

"I don't see why."

"Don't you?" Ken gestured for him to come with him. "Back in a jiff, Adrian."

"Right, Ken," the tailor said.

Julian followed Ken to another part of the store where they hung the overcoats that gave them some privacy.

Ken said, "The bearer bonds were stolen in Chicago. Have you forgotten that?"

Julian said, "No."

"They're coming here soon. Will you be ready?"

"Yes, I will. Look, Ken, the American is of no consequence. He's from Chicago, yes, but it's a coincidence."

"Is it?"

"Yes."

"Are you aware that he used to be a fucking copper?"

Julian Atherton's heart skipped a beat. Not for fear that the American was a cop, but for fear of Ken.

"What? I—"

"Ian called a friend in Chicago this morning. He was a fucking policeman, you stupid fucking sod."

"I . . . didn't . . . he was with Alistair . . ."

"Why's he with Alistair? What does he want?"

"I don't know. Probably he's a—probably he's a mate."

"A queer?"

"Yes."

"Ian doesn't think so. He's pretty fucking put out with you for bringing him right into our club."

"I didn't, Ken. He's with Alistair."

"What does he want? Huh? What does he fucking want here?"

"He's looking for a chair. A, the Tarenton chair. We were trying to do a deal. Ken, I, he's a legitimate antiques dealer. Honestly."

"Or he could be working for the American treasury department. You don't really know, do you?"

"He's not. If he is, I mean, you know, I can take care of him if it comes to that."

"You mean *we* can take care of him if it comes to that. You wouldn't know killing from your arse."

Julian Atherton was shaking with fear. A knife stuck in his throat . . .

Ken smiled. He put a meaty hand on Julian's shoulder and said, "Oh, never mind, Julian. Ian just doesn't like surprises. Right?"

". . . right. Ian—"

"Ian?"

"Ian said he used to be a cop. Is he now?"

"Well, we don't know for sure, do we? What do you think?"

"I think he knows a lot about antiques," Julian said. "He's been in the business for a long time."

"Or he could be pretending to know, working undercover for the treasury department."

"Well . . ." Julian said, his voice trailing.

Ken said, "Alright, then. Ian's going to make a few more calls, see who this bloke is. Odds are, he is who you say he is. They've already sent one treasury agent to London."

"They have?"

"Yeah. You don't know anything, do you?"

"I—"

"Never mind, Julian. You stick to the documentation, the paperwork. We'll take care of the rest."

"I shan't see him again. You needn't worry about that."

"Oh, I didn't say that. We may *need* you to see him again. Perhaps there's a place for him in all this."

Julian relaxed. He wasn't going to be killed today. "Anything you like," Julian said.

Ken said, "DeGiusti's scheduled to arrive in a couple of days. *With* the goods. Make sure you're ready."

ELEVEN

The real estate developer, whose name was Alan Shays, made a sweeping gesture with his arm and said, "We get that property condemned, see? All of it. Then we knock it down, replace it with warehouses."

Shays and Ian Shivers stood before a row of brown two-story buildings, molded and decayed. Their fancy cars looked out of place in the slum. Down the road a couple of black kids stood on a corner.

Ian Shivers said, "What sort of financing you after?"

"We get the buildings condemned, then we apply for a government loan. nonrecourse. Submit a development plan. Simple."

Ian said, "I mean, what sort of financing you seeking from us?"

Shays said, "I was thinking about one, one point two million, cash. Get the condemnation, get the loan. One two three. In three years, you get your money back five times."

"That's six million pounds."

"Right."

"We may hold you to that, Alan."

"Alright," Shays said. "But I'll need your help in other ways."

"What other ways would that be?"

"Your contacts in Parliament."

Ian Shivers smiled. His smile gleamed, his teeth even and white and decidedly un-British. Like many wealthy Britons in the public eye, he had spent good money having his teeth fixed. Ian said, "What would you know about that?"

The real estate developer flushed. Lord Melvey's relationship with Ken Shivers was well known throughout the London underground. But it wasn't polite to discuss it openly. Certainly not in front of the Shivers.

"No disrespect intended, Ian," Shays said. "But every little bit helps."

" 'Course," Ian said.

His cell phone rang.

"Excuse me," Ian said. He walked away and answered the call.

"Yeah."

"Ian?" An American voice, a Chicago accent. It was Eddie Salvetti.

"Yeah? How are you, mate?"

"I'm okay," Salvetti said. "I checked into that guy for you."

"What'd you learn?"

"He's not a cop anymore. He was forced out years ago after he killed a drug dealer. Chicago PD suspected him of taking money from the dealer and killing him to cover it up."

"That so?"

"Yeah. And last year he had a run-in with these Chinkos running most of the local heroin. He may have whacked a couple of them. Chicago PD investigated him on that too, but couldn't make anything stick."

"Sounds like a regular menace, he does."

"He can be. But I don't think he's a crook, Ian. He used to do some bounty hunting. You know, chase after guys that skipped out on bond after their arrest."

"A mercenary."

"In a way."

"What's he doing here then?"

71

"Probably what he says he's doing. Looking for an antique. I wouldn't worry about him. He's a nobody."

Ian said, "He's taken blokes down, though. Permanent like."

"Yeah, but he's not the kind that goes looking for trouble. Word is, here, if the mob's involved, he steers clear. We've never had any problem with him."

"Maybe it's because you're not Chinese."

"I doubt that. He went after them because they went after a friend of his. A woman friend. She was Italian."

"An Italian bird, eh? One of yours?"

"No. Not one of ours."

Down the road, a red vintage Jaguar MK II came around the corner. Cliff Wilkinson and Kenny approaching.

Ian said, "I get the feeling if this fellah were to disappear, the Chicago police might be grateful."

"Well, I'm not going to encourage that. You do what you want to do, but I don't want to know about it. Okay?"

"Alright, Eddie. Ciao."

Kenny and Cliff stepped out of the red Jag. Kenny moved over to Alan and threw a couple of fake punches, boxing with him, Alan lifting his hands up, laughing at the Kenny Shivers greeting, trying to hide his fear. Cliff Wilkinson mopped the top of Alan's head, messing up his moussed hair. Alan took it with an affected good nature. He had made his bargain and he knew it. The Shivers frightened him, but he needed their money.

Ian said, "Ken, come here."

Ken threw another left jab, this one making contact with Alan's shoulder, smarting though not bruising. Ken walked over to his brother.

Ian started walking down the road, Ken beside him.

Ian said, "Just got off the phone with Eddie." He told him what Eddie had said.

Ken said, "You think Maitland's a copper?"

72

"No. I think he's got business with Alistair. Or Julian and Julian's not telling us."

"Maybe we should have a talk with Julian."

"Not that sort of talk," Ian said. "We need him in good spirits till this job is done."

"Alright," Ken said. "What's Alan want, then?"

"Million pounds and change. Says we'll get it back five times."

Ken looked at the shabby row houses on their left. "Knock down this lot?"

"Yeah," Ian said. "Needs to have it condemned."

"I'll talk to Melvey," Ken said. "Had supper yet?"

"No."

"Want to get a bite at the club?"

"Can't," Ian said. "I'm meeting Doreen."

"Christ," Ken said. "What you want with a fuckin' woman? They smell and they give you diseases."

"Part of the good life," Ian said.

"Suit yourself, then." Ken stopped. About twenty yards away, the two black teenagers were staring at them sullenly. Ken stared back. Moments slowly passed. The black kids walked away.

"Disgraceful," Ken said and spat on the ground. Then he turned and started to walk back to the Jaguar.

Ian stayed and watched the black kids walking away. Ken had wanted to start something with them. He had asked for it. If it had happened, Ian would have backed him. Maybe smashed the kids' heads into the curb if it had come to it. Ian would always back Ken. Even when Ken would start fights unnecessarily. Like a kid.

But we aren't kids anymore, Ian thought. Christ, they weren't even young. Forty coming up and he had no family. His mum and his brother. That was it. Kenny was content to live the rest of his days banging nineteen-year-old boys and cutting up people's faces. Kenny didn't think about the future.

Ian was keeping something from his brother. The truth was, he was getting serious with Doreen. They were talking about getting married and raising a family. Christ, he had to think about the future. Building businesses, gaining respect in the community, breaking away from Thursday dinners with mum. Things had to change. Kenny would have to understand that.

Earlier today he had considered telling Kenny his plans with Doreen. But then he decided he would tell him later. After the present business was taken care of. The bearer bonds, Julian's work on the forged certificates, the American treasury agent.

And the other American. The other one from Chicago.

Kenny was bonkers, but he wasn't bloody stupid. Kenny had said maybe there was a place for Maitland in all this. Maybe he was right.

TWELVE

It was around one in the morning when Maitland got out of bed. His breath was fogging. It was that cold. He wondered if the heating system had broken down. At his apartment in Chicago, he usually set the thermostat down to sixty-three degrees Fahrenheit in the winter. Here in this English bedroom he wondered if the temperature was even forty. He didn't want to wake up the old woman to see if something was wrong. Eventually, he went into his suitcase and put on a pair of jeans, a sweatshirt and socks. He tried to remember if he had brought a hat. Then decided he hadn't. He got back in bed and went back to sleep.

Daylight came and he got out of bed. He undressed and pulled on a bathrobe, took his shaving kit and went to the bathroom. He took a hot shower and tried not to think about hypothermia.

In the kitchen, Mrs. Cavendish gave him a friendly good morning. She wore a pink and yellow nightgown and slippers. She said, "Would you like some breakfast?"

Maitland saw toast covered with some sort of brown sauce he'd never seen before.

"Oh, not much of a breakfast eater," he said. "Do you have any coffee?"

" 'Course. Have a seat."

He sat down at the small table with the red vinyl top.

The coffee was weak—she had probably used half measures.

But they fell into easy conversation. Maitland learned that she had been a nurse at the Cheam hospital and had married a banker who had died five years earlier. They talked about Princess Diana and the London trains and the Queen Mum's fondness for gin. She told him she had a daughter in Cornwall and a son in Islington. She asked him a few polite questions about his work and his home and whether or not he had a family. Maitland liked her. She was kind and unpretentious and unaffected. Yet she seemed neither lonely nor needy. Apart from grumbling about traffic, she didn't complain about anything. He decided not to say anything about the lack of heat.

He left the house and drove to a café two miles away. He ordered bacon, eggs, buttered toast and juice and coffee with milk. He felt better after the meal.

It took him an hour to drive to the Waring Hotel. The clerk at the front desk told him there were no messages for him.

The clerk gave him an odd look and said, "Are you checking out, sir?"

"No," Maitland said.

"As you wish," the clerk said. And Maitland knew the clerk knew he had spent the night elsewhere.

He passed the next couple of hours at the British Museum. It lost its charm somewhere near the Townely Sculptures and he decided he would go to the war museum instead or to a movie. But before he got to the tube his cell phone rang.

"Maitland."

"Yes, Julian here. I think we may be able to help you. Can you meet me this evening?"

"Sure. Where and when?"

"There's a flat in Bethnal Green. That's in the East End. Four-twelve Vallance Road. Nine o'clock."

"Okay," Maitland said. "I'll see you then."

THIRTEEN

Maitland had turned on the brights because the night was so foggy, but eventually realized he could see better with the lights on regular beam. The old Ford didn't have fog lights. A few days in London and it had been foggy every night, overcast and gray every day. Not seeing blue sky and sun was starting to wear on his psyche. He wondered if it depressed the locals.

He found Vallance Road, but had trouble reading the numbers on the houses. All the houses seemed the same. In time he discerned a number on a house and worked backward and found the right address.

There was a light in the window on the second floor. Nothing on the first.

Maitland parked the car around the corner and walked to the doorstep. He looked down the narrow road both ways. He didn't see far for the fog. He rang the doorbell.

A light came on inside and he saw a stairwell inside. A man descended the stairs. Julian Atherton.

Julian said, "Good evening."

Maitland followed Julian up the stairs and into a small sitting room. The furniture was drab, the room dim. The only source of light in the room was from a lamp on top of an empty bookshelf. In front of a black, squarish leather sofa there was a narrow coffee table with a bottle of whisky and a couple of glasses. There was an old radio sitting on the windowsill, Paul Anka singing *Lonely Boy.*

"Drink?" Julian said.

"No thanks," Maitland said. "Are we waiting for someone?"

"Yes," Julian said. "The seller."

"He's agreed to meet with us, then?"

"Yes. Of course, he doesn't live here. He still wishes to keep this transaction discreet."

"Why?"

Julian said, "Ask him. When he arrives." Julian poured two fingers of whisky into a glass. No ice.

He sat down and said, "How has your stay been?"

"Okay," Maitland said.

"You're at the Hilton, correct?"

"No. The Waring."

"Ah. Nice digs."

"Yes, it's very accommodating."

"Yes, the Waring has been in business for—" A cell phone rang. Julian's. He excused himself and answered it.

Maitland heard him say: "Yes . . . yes, he's here now. . . . Pardon?" Julian sighed. He stood up and made an apologetic gesture to Maitland. "Excuse me," Julian said and moved out of the room.

He was gone a while and then Maitland heard the door downstairs open. Then he heard footsteps coming up the stairs. More than one set of footsteps. They drew closer. Maitland stood up and moved near the door to the sitting room.

The first man to reach the top of the stairs and come into his view was compact and dressed in a suit. His hair cut short and conservatively. A Republican delegate or an FBI agent, Maitland thought. Whatever he was, he looked like an American.

The man behind him was a head taller, big and wide, with a bushy mustache and hair that came down over his ears.

The short one said, "Hello."

And now Maitland knew he was an American.

"Hello," Maitland said, his tone wary.

The short man said, "Joe Roddy. United States Treasury. What's your name?"

Shit, Maitland thought. A fucking American federal agent. He did not like this one bit. What were they setting him up for?

Maitland called out, "Atherton. Come out here."

No answer.

"Atherton," Maitland said. "Come here. I want to talk to you."

Maitland looked down the corridor. A door opened and a man stepped out. The man was wearing a black overcoat. Maitland recognized him from before. He started to say something and Ian Shivers took a Browning automatic out of his pocket and pointed it at Joe Roddy. Maitland's eyes went wide and he got out, "Hey—!" and Ian Shivers shot Joe Roddy twice in the chest. Joe Roddy fell to the floor and Ian walked over to him and shot him in the head.

Shivers bent over Roddy's corpse and took his service weapon out of his holster. The service weapon was a Glock .40 caliber. Shivers handed the Glock to Sergeant Bill Raines. Now Maitland saw that Shivers was wearing white latex gloves. Shivers held the Browning on Maitland and said, "We meet again." Shivers smiled.

Maitland said, "You killed a cop."

"No, you did," Ian said. He turned to the sergeant from Scotland Yard and said, "Go ahead, Bill."

Sergeant Raines looked at Maitland then at Ian Shivers. He had been told the plan but he had not been told this part. No one had told him he would be expected to kill anyone himself. Sergeant Raines had never killed anyone. Not directly.

He said, "What?"

"Go ahead," Ian said. "Do him."

". . . Ian."

Maitland stepped once. Closer to the lamp. Stepped again. "Christ, Ian, I never . . . I can't."

"Oh, bloody hell," Ian said and took the Glock back from the sergeant. That was when Maitland grabbed the lamp and yanked its cord from the wall. The room went dark. Voices cried out in protest and Maitland rushed to the door, his arms in front of him. He made contact with someone and knocked them back. A flash of gunfire lit up the room. Then two more shots and then Maitland was running down the stairs. The stairwell was dark too, but not as dark as the room and he kept his footing as he went down and there was another gunshot before he burst through the front door.

He got to the street and saw a red Jaguar coming toward him. The Jag came to a stop and a man said through the window, "Oy. Come here."

But the man behind the voice looked very much like the man who had killed the fed. *His brother,* Maitland thought, and ran.

There were parked cars between Maitland and the street, protecting him from being shot by the men inside the Jaguar. When there were spaces between the cars, the Jaguar would swerve into the curb, trying to run him down but then Maitland would run past the gap and the Jaguar would be forced to swerve back out.

But he was running out of street, the end of the block coming up and the Jaguar sped up and made a sharp turn in front of him and screeched to a stop and the driver was getting out and Maitland rushed forward, timing it right, as the driver stepped between the door and the car and Maitland hit the door and smashed it into the driver. The driver slumped down and Maitland slammed the door again. The glass shattered against the driver's head. The driver slipped to the ground. Maitland kicked him twice, the second time in the balls.

Ken Shivers was in the passenger seat. He scooted over with

something in his hand. Maitland saw the knife in Ken's hand. He grabbed Ken's wrist and pulled it through the door. Then he slammed the door against the wrist. Ken cried out, dropping the knife. Maitland kicked the knife underneath the car and then ran.

He got back to the Ford, started it and drove away.

FOURTEEN

Ian said, "Christ, what's happened here?"

Cliff Wilkinson was still on the ground clutching his testicles. Kenny held his own hand. Sergeant Raines held the American agent's gun and Ian still had the Browning and the latex gloves.

Kenny said, "He escaped."

"How?" Ian said.

"He drove off in a fucking car, you fucking sod," Ken said. "Where the hell were you?"

An argument ensued. Brothers shouting at the tops of their voices, exchanging foul language, frequently calling each other the c-word as some Brits do.

Sergeant Raines interrupted, saying, "We can't stay here."

"Shut up," Ian said. To Ken he said, "Get Cliff into the car. You," he said, turning to the policeman, "call your people, report a murder. And a suspect."

Things were moving too fast for Detective Sergeant Bill Raines. The injuries to Ken and Cliff, the broken glass on the street. Raines said, "But—"

"*Now,*" Ian said.

Cliff Wilkinson was loaded into the back of the Jaguar. Ken got behind the wheel and Ian walked around to the passenger side.

Ian said across the roof of the car, "It's alright, Bill. You've still got your suspect. Like as not, we'll find him before they do. If we don't, the coppers will handle him."

"Ian—"

"See you later," Ian said.

The Jaguar sped away. Sergeant Raines watched it disappear into the fog. He walked back to the house. He switched on the light in the stairwell and walked up. Part of him hoped that none of this had happened, but he got upstairs and found the hallway switch and saw the American agent's body on the floor. He picked up the lamp and plugged it back in. He spent the next few minutes looking over the room, getting his story straight. Then he called Inspector Martin on his cell phone.

"It's Bill. . . . Bad. Agent Roddy's been killed . . . no, no need for Armed Response. The shooter got away."

Inspector Martin, "Oh hell. Do you know who the shooter was?"

"His name is Maitland. An American, from Chicago."

FIFTEEN

Maitland parked the car in the garage behind Mrs. Cavendish's house. He made sure the garage door was closed and then he walked around to the front of the house.

The living room was empty. Mrs. Cavendish was upstairs sleeping. Maitland searched the kitchen for liquor and found a bottle of Bushmills. Protestant whiskey. He poured some into a glass and drank it down. He looked at his watch. Then he called his lawyer.

His lawyer was Sam Stillman. A bantam rooster of a man, small of stature and big-headed, like an actor. Sam had been a prosecutor before being a criminal defense attorney. Maitland had brought one of Sam's clients back from Kansas when the client had jumped bond. The client turned out to be not guilty, which wasn't common. That was how Maitland met Sam Stillman. He had used Sam a couple of times after that.

It was afternoon in Chicago and Sam was in his office. When he answered the phone, he said, "Okay, now what have you done?" Being humorous.

Maitland told him what happened. Sam went into lawyer mode, listening patiently when necessary, asking questions when he had to. No more jokes.

When Maitland was finished, Sam said, "Have you called the police?"

"No."

"Christ, Evan. Why not?"

"I don't know. I got away and I was so scared they were behind me. That they'd catch up to me. It was a half hour before I let myself think I lost them. Then I came back here."

"Where are you staying?"

"At a bed and breakfast in South London."

"I thought you said you'd checked into the Waring?"

"I did. I'm still registered there, in fact."

"Why did you move?"

"I don't know." Maitland said, "I had a feeling."

"What?"

"Well, when I got here I met with Lethbridge, he gave me a bad feeling. He seemed dangerous. Or, he seemed to surround himself with dangerous people. Anyway, I just had a feeling and I acted on it."

"Okay, and you were right," the lawyer said. "But it's not going to look good, Evan. It'll look like you're being cagey."

"As opposed to cautious?"

"Hey, I'm on your side."

"I know, Sam. I'm sorry."

"Forget it. But you still haven't told me why you haven't called the police."

"A couple of reasons. One, I don't know the procedure here. I don't know if I'm entitled to have a lawyer. Whether or not I have Fifth Amendment rights, etc."

"You don't. You're not in the States."

"Oh."

"What's the other reason?"

"The other reason is I'm pretty sure I'm being set up."

"Well . . . yeah."

"No, I mean set up for murder. The guy who shot the treasury agent, his name was Ian. I don't know his last name. But I saw him before. At a restaurant. Wait a minute; it was *his* restaurant. It belonged to him and his brother. And they knew Julian Ather-

ton and Lethbridge. When Ian shot the agent, he was wearing
latex gloves. They were going to shoot me—the guy he was
with—he was supposed to shoot me. And then they were going
to pin the agent's murder on me."

"But you'd be dead?"

"Yeah, Sam, that's the idea. I'd be dead and they'd claim
self-defense."

"Who was the other guy?"

"I don't know. Ian called him Bill."

"Bill."

"Yeah, Bill. That's all I got."

"You said something earlier. 'You killed him.' "

"No, I said to Ian, 'You killed a cop.' And he said, 'No, you
did.' That was it."

Silence on the telephone.

"Well, Sam," Maitland said, "what do you suggest?"

Stillman said, "I've got a trial day after tomorrow. I think I
can get a continuance and catch a flight to London. But if I
request one, I'll have to tell the judge why. And I don't lie to
judges."

"I wouldn't ask you to."

"What I'm saying is, my activity here might tip people off
that you're in trouble. And it does involve a Chicago federal
agent."

"Yeah. What do you think would happen if Chicago PD got
wind of this?"

"I think they'd be very happy. At least some of them would."

"I'm not a criminal."

"Doesn't matter," Stillman said. "Not to your enemies at the
PD. Phone calls will be made. *What about this guy Maitland?
Oh, he's a piece of shit. No doubt he killed that fed.* If you somehow
get out of England, they'll transport you back."

"So I can't leave?"

86

"I didn't say that. I . . ." Stillman's voice trailed off.

"What then?"

"The best thing to do," Stillman said, "is to get a lawyer there and get it resolved there. Tell the police what happened. Give me a couple of hours and I'll find a lawyer you can call there."

"And hope for the best."

"Yeah." Stillman didn't seem too confident.

Another silence.

Then the lawyer said, "You're not going to do that, are you?"

"I don't know, Sam. What you're saying is probably good advice. But . . . I don't know."

"Evan, sometimes you have to trust the system."

"I used to trust the system. Then a couple of Chicago cops tried to pin a murder on me."

"That was years ago."

"Well, it's still with me. And people are still after me."

"Here or there?"

"Both places," Maitland said. He smiled bitterly. "Do I sound paranoid?"

"Kind of."

"Alright, Sam. I'll call the police."

"I'll make some calls, line you up with a lawyer. Okay?"

"Yeah. Thanks, Sam." Maitland gave him his cell number and they said goodbye.

Sixteen

He wanted to feel better in the morning. But he didn't. He woke up after a fitful night in a cold room and the problem was still with him. It played out again in his mind: the American agent saying his name, the Cockney gangster coming down the hall with the gun in his latexed hand, the agent getting shot and killed. Maitland had witnessed it all.

So what? What if the man wasn't an American agent? What if he had been lying? What did it have to do with him? Couldn't he just stay out of it?

But then Maitland thought of the American agent. Compact, stiff, upright. He looked like a fed. Even before he had identified himself as an American treasury agent, Maitland had thought he had looked like a fed. Roddy was the sort the federal agencies liked. He probably had a family back home. Did he deserve to be forgotten?

No, you did.

They were going to frame him for Roddy's murder. Kill him and put a gun in his dead hand. The one called Ian had given the agent's gun to the big guy. Telling him, "Go ahead. Do him." Shoot him.

Shoot me, Maitland thought. They were going to do it too. Of that he had no doubt.

Or rather, Ian was going to do it. The big one had hesitated. Probably he had never killed anyone before. His hesitation had bought Maitland some time. Maybe he would thank the guy for that if he ever saw him again. Thank him after he threw him down a flight of stairs.

Or maybe he would drive straight to the airport, get on a plane and fly home. Hope that nobody would stop him. *Mr. Maitland? We have some questions for you* . . . Get on a plane and go home and tell Max Glendenning to content himself with one chair. Who was Joe Roddy to him? What did he owe him?

"Shit," Maitland said.

He backed the Ford out of the garage and began the drive to the Waring Hotel. He would call Scotland Yard from there.

He felt better when he made the decision. It wouldn't be easy. A foreign country, witness to a murder, questions about what he was doing there . . . but he knew some things. The man called Ian, Alastair Lethbridge, Julian Atherton. Odds were all three of them had had some previous run-ins with the law and were familiar to the local police. Let them bring those three in for questioning and see what they turned up.

When Maitland had been the subject of an internal investigation when he was a cop, his lawyer had asked him, "Do you think you did anything wrong?"

Maitland had answered he did not.

"Then you have nothing to hide."

Maitland parked the car a block away from the Waring.

He walked toward the hotel and stopped when he saw a police car out front. A marked unit with lights on top. Another four-door unmarked unit behind it.

Maitland stopped.

He saw four, maybe five uniformed officers and a couple of plainclothesman. Then he saw a big man with a mustache walk out of the hotel lobby.

The man with the federal agent. The man who wouldn't shoot him on Ian's orders.

Now the man wasn't in handcuffs. Now he saw the man walk

up to one of the uniformed police officers. The uniformed officer said something to the big man and the big man laughed. The uniformed officer handed the big man a cigarette.

Christ. He's a cop.

Maitland turned, feigning interest in a newspaper stand. He avoided sudden movements. Then he walked away.

He got into the Ford and drove away.

Inspector Martin came out of the hotel and walked over to Sergeant Raines.

"They haven't seen him since yesterday. They said he hasn't spent the night at the hotel for the last two nights."

Raines said, "He check out?"

"No," Martin said. "That's the funny thing. He hasn't checked out."

"Cagey," Raines said. "Probably he's tried to leave town."

"Airports are blocked," Martin said. "He's not going anywhere." Martin glanced at the uniformed cop then back at Raines. Martin gestured for Raines to walk away with him so they could speak privately.

DI Martin looked at the cigarette dangling from Raines's lip. Martin said, "Thought you quit smoking."

"I did," Raines said. "Kind of nervous, you know. It was a shock, seeing that."

"I'm sure it was. What was this Maitland doing in London?"

"Roddy said he was a bad character from Chicago. He said he believed he was here to help bring the stolen securities."

"How did Roddy know about him?"

"Like I said, they're both from Chicago."

"No, I mean, how did Roddy know Maitland was tied in with the stolen securities?"

"He never told me."

Martin said, "He never told me either."

Inspector Martin let it hang out there. Raines said nothing. Martin said, "Why didn't you call me?"

"I did."

"*Before* you went to the East End."

"We already talked about this."

"I know," Martin said. "But soon we'll have to talk about this again with FBI agents. And probably some blokes from the Treasury Department. I want to get it straight."

"I told you," Raines said, "it was Roddy's idea to go. He asked me to come with him."

"You should have told me," Martin said. "I would have come with you."

"Okay, I should have told you."

"Why did he call you? I'm senior officer. Why did he call you instead of me?"

"I don't know. He said he felt comfortable with me."

"He hardly knew you."

"Christ, Ronnie. I can't speak for him. The geezer's dead. What do you want me to do? I can't fucking go back in time. I can't change it."

"We're supposed to meet with the DCI today."

"Is he put out with me?"

"He's put out with both of us."

In the street, black Austin cabs went by. A red double-decker bus stopped, an advertisement for Sky News network on the side.

Raines said, "I'm sorry, Ronnie. I had no idea that would happen."

Inspector Martin wanted to hit the younger sergeant. He had always liked Bill Raines, but he thought now that Bill wasn't being entirely truthful with him. A dead American agent on their hands and more American agents on the way. The FBI would be demanding answers in more detail than Bill had given so far.

A lot more detail. Their DCI had told them they were to give full cooperation to the Americans. And after that was done, the DCI said, he would deal with them himself. Christ, they'd be lucky to keep their pensions.

SEVENTEEN

Maitland drove to Kensington. He stopped at an ice cream shop and ordered coffee and asked if they had a telephone book. He found Alistair Lethbridge's telephone number and address in the professional listings under dentistry.

The waiting room of the dentist's office was fitted with Danish furniture, blond wood frames and pale covers. *Ok* and British *Esquire* magazines on the side tables. On the wall, a Modigliani print.

There were three patients in the waiting room. A middle-aged woman and a posh young man and woman.

The receptionist was a honey-haired girl of about twenty. She wore a mini-skirt with black tights and a white sweater. She asked Maitland if he had an appointment.

Maitland said he didn't.

"What's your name?" the receptionist asked.

"Terry," Maitland said. He did not make his voice effeminate, but his tone was needy and perhaps even desperate. He said, "I met Alistair the other night. I just want to tell him something."

The girl rolled her eyes at this American poof. She said, "He's working now; he's got patients lined up till four. You can't . . . you can't come here like this and expect to see him."

"Can't he take a break?"

"No. He'll be done by four. Please, sir. You can't hang about here."

"Fine," Maitland said and walked out. As he passed, the

93

middle-aged woman glanced at him and shook her head and went back to reading her magazine.

Maitland waited in the car. At twelve minutes after four, Alistair Lethbridge came out of his office and got into his blue Rover. Maitland started the Ford Granada and followed him. After a series of turns Maitland had no idea of east and west and did not know if Lethbridge was driving to his home or elsewhere. Maitland suspected elsewhere.

He was right. About a half hour later they were on a narrow road in what Maitland believed was South London. The sun was gone and the gray was chased out by dark. Maitland watched Lethbridge park the Rover and walk into a club with no sign.

Maitland parked the Ford and walked into the club. It was dark and dirty inside. The bar was L-shaped. A large room bordered the long side of the bar, a smaller, somewhat enclosed room that was even darker than the main room. There were a few men in there, shadows standing close to each other. On the jukebox, Morrissey was singing *Meat is Murder.* Behind the bar, the bartender looked at Maitland, sized him up, and gave him an unfriendly frown. Maitland could fool a young girl, but he couldn't fool this guy.

"Can I help you, sir?" the bartender said, his tone unwelcoming. As if Maitland was a cop.

"Looking for my mother," Maitland said.

Now he saw Alistair Lethbridge sitting in a booth with a young long-haired man. Lethbridge looked at him, his expression angry. He made no effort to move.

The bartender said, "Very funny. Will you be having a drink?"

"Half pint of bitters."

"In a thin glass?" the bartender said.

"Sure," Maitland said. He looked back at Lethbridge. The

bartender placed the glass on the bar and Maitland paid for it, leaving a generous tip. The bartender swiped up the cash without saying anything.

Maitland walked over to the table. The young man looked up at him. He said, "Who's this geezer?"

"Get a haircut," Maitland said. To Lethbridge he said, "Surprised to see me?"

"A little, yes," Lethbridge said. "I thought you were finished with me."

Maitland studied him for a moment. He wondered how good a liar Lethbridge was. Now he wondered if he knew what Julian had done to him.

Maitland said, "Maybe you thought you were finished with me."

The long hair said, "What's going on?"

Lethbridge sighed and said, "Go away, Tony. I'll chat with you later."

Tony left and Maitland took a seat.

Lethbridge said, "Why are you following me, old boy?"

"Don't you know?"

"No."

"Where's Julian?"

"Julian? How should I know?"

"I'd like to speak to him," Maitland said.

"Then speak to him. I'm out of it."

Was he out of it? Maitland thought. Maitland said, "What about Ian?"

Lethbridge paled a little. He said, "Ian Shivers?"

"Yeah," Maitland said. "The guy we met at dinner the other night."

Lethbridge said, "Ian's got no part in your business. It's Julian's deal."

"What about his brother?"

95

"Kenny's not interested in antiques." Lethbridge frowned. "Why are you asking about the Shivers?"

"I'm curious."

"Well, let me give you some advice, sunshine. Don't go nosing about the Shivers. They're the top mobsters in London. Cross them and they'll cut you up into little pieces."

"You mean they'd kill me."

"And not think twice," Lethbridge said. "They like it, you see. They get pleasure delivering pain."

"I'll remember that."

A thin man in his forties came in wearing a Playboy bunny suit. He had a cigarette dangling from his mouth. He sat at the bar and shook hands with the bartender.

Maitland said, "What about the Tarenton chair?"

"I told you," Lethbridge said, "I'm out of it. It's between you and Julian now. He's the fixer."

"But you were the one that contacted Glendenning. Not Julian."

"I was not authorized to do that. I'm out now."

"Who *is* Julian Atherton?"

"What do you mean?"

"I mean, what is he? What does he do? Is he a lawyer, what?"

"Nobody really knows. He was in Hong Kong for a time, before the reversion. He came back with a pile of money. Now he owns a bank, an insurance company, a lot of nice cars. He owns a mansion in Surrey, near Box Hill. He has another home on the Italian Riviera."

"He's rich."

"Very. And well protected."

"Where's the mansion in Surrey?"

"Twelve Napier Road. But I wouldn't bother him if I were you. He's got friends."

"You don't say," Maitland said. "Tell me the name of the

man who owns the chair. I'll pay you for the information. We don't have to go through Atherton."

"No chance. I'm out."

"Are you afraid of Julian?"

Lethbridge sipped his drink.

Maitland said, "Are you afraid of the Shivers?"

Lethbridge looked at him.

Maitland said, "Does Julian work for the Shivers?"

"That's none of your business."

"Does he work *with* them?"

Lethbridge raised a palm, shook his head.

"I'm entitled to know."

"You're entitled to nothing," Lethbridge said. "Forget Julian, Maitland. Forget the bloody chair. Get on a plane and get the hell out of London. I'm warning you."

"I wished you'd warned me before."

"Excuse me?"

"Nothing," Maitland said. He stood up. "I'll see you around, Lethbridge."

In the car, Maitland took the notebook out of his jacket pocket. He wrote down the names of Julian Atherton, Ian Shivers, and Ken Shivers.

EIGHTEEN

The road was narrow and bordered by tall hedges. Maitland didn't think he'd ever been on such a narrow road. He didn't think it was possible to do a U-turn. If a car came from the other direction, you'd have to pull off and scrape the side of the car up against a hedge. It was beautiful and mysterious but it intimidated and disoriented him and he didn't need anymore of that right now.

The street numbers were hard to see too. Lethbridge had given him the address, but there were no well-lighted places telling you where the number was. As if they didn't want strangers to find it.

At one point, Maitland believed he had overshot number twelve. An iron gate in the hedge. He stopped the car and backed up and got out and walked up to the gate. The gate was locked but it had a barely discernable number 12 written on the border.

Maitland got back in the car and drove up the road about a quarter mile. He found a patch of ground off the road and parked the car. Then he walked back to the gate.

By the time he got there his eyes had adjusted as best they could to the darkness and the fog. The gate was bordered by stone walls about seven feet high, the walls covered by ivy. Maitland jumped up and grabbed the top of the wall, got a foot against the wall and pulled himself to the top. He got one leg over and then the other. He looked at the ground on the other side then jumped down.

He saw the house ahead. It was indeed a mansion. Not palatial, but high dollar. Probably eight to ten million dollars for the spread. The house was three floors, white stone with dark brown borders. A driveway ran from the gate to the front of the house, semicircling the front door and continuing around to a three-car garage, which had once been a horse stable. Tall trees ran up both sides of the grounds. There was a vintage Mercedes 600 limousine near the front door. Maitland wondered if he'd seen the car before.

He kept to the side, walking by the trees, and circled around to the back of the house. He stayed in the shadows and watched.

Light poured out from three sets of windows. One room was a kitchen, the second window a bathroom, the third and largest was a living room. Maitland waited and in a moment saw movement. A slight Asian woman wearing a purple robe, holding a glass of wine. Then another person in a matching purple robe. A man with long hair and glasses. The man was not Julian Atherton.

Maitland waited another ten minutes. He saw the man and the woman move to a couch. The woman tucked her legs up beneath her and the man bent over the coffee table, putting his head over it. A second or two passed and he lifted his head up, exhilarated. Maitland decided the man had just snorted a line of cocaine. He said, "Shit," and moved to the back of the house. It was too cold outside.

He came in through the door to the kitchen. When he was inside he heard music. Dean Martin singing *Mambo Italiano*. There was no one in the kitchen. He moved quietly, out of the kitchen, through the hall as the music's volume increased . . . *hey Cadrule, you don't ah have to go school* . . . then he heard a crack.

Maitland stopped.

Another crack.

A man's voice, groaning.

Maitland moved to the living room door. He opened it. The couple inside did not notice him. The man was bent over the coffee table, his purple bathrobe hiked up over his waist. The woman hit him again with a horse's riding crop and the man gave another cry. Maitland was at once disgusted and amused.

The woman heard him laugh.

"Who are you?" she said.

"A guest," Maitland said.

The man looked up from the coffee table. It was like he was strapped over a horse's back. He did not seem embarrassed. He said, "You want to join in?"

"No, I do not. Can you . . . ?" Maitland made a gesture to the man's rear end. He didn't want to see it.

The man stood up and his robe fell down so that he was no longer exposed.

"Suit yerself," the man said.

Maitland came into the room. He said, "I'm looking for Julian. Is he here?"

"No," the long-haired man said. "He gave us the house for the weekend."

"Do you know where he is?"

"Probably at his flat in London. You a friend?"

"Yeah," Maitland said.

The Asian woman looked at him with contempt. She held the riding crop by her side. She said, "Who asked you here?"

She moved toward him, coming from the side.

"No one," Maitland said. Then she hit him across the face with the riding crop.

It shocked him more than hurt him, though he still felt the sting across his face. She raised it to hit him again but this time he was ready and he caught it with his left hand. She was small and light and it was easy to pull her in. He yanked the crop out of her hand and pushed her back.

The woman said, "You bully."

Maitland touched his own face. No blood, but a welt had risen. He said, "What the hell's the matter with you?"

"I'm Vietnamese," she said. "We are a fighting people."

The long-haired man smiled and said, "She's a tough bird, isn't she?" Proud of her, apparently. "Ran you lot out of Saigon, didn't she?"

"She wasn't even alive then, you idiot."

The man looked at Maitland, stoned and disoriented. He smiled stupidly.

Maitland said, "Do you expect Julian back anytime soon?"

". . . who?"

"Ju—oh fuck, never mind."

Maitland turned to go. But then he looked at the Vietnamese woman getting something out of her bag. It was a gun and now she was pointing it at him. A wild look in her eye.

Maitland looked at the gun. It was real. A Colt 1911 .45. An expensive gun. Hopefully not loaded and if loaded, hopefully not chambered and ready.

Maitland said, "Alright, alright. I'm leaving. Okay?"

"You're not leaving," she said. "We're not through with you."

Maitland said, "Now I know you don't want to hurt anyone. And I'm going. So why don't you put that down?"

She pulled the trigger, proving it *was* loaded and chambered. The gunshot echoed in the room as the bullet went past Maitland and into a grand piano. She pulled the trigger again and shattered the back window of the house. Before she could pull it a third time Maitland closed the distance between them and brought the riding crop down on her wrist. She cried out and dropped the gun. The man with the glasses ran to pick it up but Maitland kicked it away from him. The man with the

101

glasses grabbed Maitland by the shoulders. He was taller than Maitland but he was pale and thin and probably sick. Maitland punched him hard in the solar plexus and the man fell to his knees, gasping and coughing. Then Maitland picked up the gun.

He looked at the Vietnamese woman across the room and she looked back at him. Now he held the gun in one hand and the riding crop in the other. The woman smiled at him then and he believed that creeped him out more than anything.

She said, "You sure you don't want to stay?"

"With the undead?" Maitland said. "No, I'll pass."

He put the gun in his coat pocket and walked out. When he got outside he threw the riding crop away.

NINETEEN

Maitland drove back to Mrs. Cavendish's bed and breakfast. Mrs. Cavendish was upstairs, asleep. Maitland turned on the television in the living room. He flipped through the channels until he found the news. He saw nothing about the murder of an American federal agent.

If it had happened in the States, it would have been on the news. If a city cop had been murdered, it would have been front and center. Even in a city the size of Chicago. The chief of police would have expressed deep sorrow and declared that every resource would be used to apprehend the cop killer.

But Maitland wasn't in the States. He was in England.

If he could get to Julian Atherton and question him. What had Atherton done to him? Why?

Maitland wondered if he was any better off now than he was this morning. He decided that he wasn't. Now he was wanted by the police. Now he knew that the big man with Ian Shivers was a cop. A dirty cop in league with a gangster named Ian Shivers. A dirty cop in a position to frame him. They were all on the same team: Shivers, Atherton, the cop.

They knew who Maitland was. They probably knew what he was. An ex-cop from Chicago with a cloudy past. Accusations of murdering a witness, accusations of taking money from a drug dealer. They had picked a good mark.

Maitland thought back to that scene at Julian Atherton's mansion. The freaky, stone-assed couple, the woman shooting

103

rounds out of a .45 . . . crazy. Julian had probably made money dealing drugs at one time. Maybe he still was. Julian had set him up.

Maitland had a gun now and that was something. But now he wondered if going to Atherton's house had been a good idea. If they were smart, they would have been waiting for him there. And when he thought "they," he didn't think of the police. He thought of the Shivers. The Shivers probably wouldn't want Atherton mixed up in it. Atherton had been used to draw Maitland in. They wouldn't want Maitland around as a witness.

Indeed, they wouldn't want Maitland as a witness either. They'd want him dead.

What was it that asshole cop had said to him years ago?

Maitland had killed a drug dealer in self-defense. And the internal affairs investigator—a chicken-shit prick named Terry Specht—had tried to show Maitland had done it without provocation. Maitland had said, "You have no evidence to support that."

Specht said, "Right. You murdered our chief witness."

It was one of many things Specht had said to try to rile him. To try to get him to come across the table and punch him in the face . . . draw a charge for assault upon an officer. But Maitland controlled himself. He knew he was innocent.

But if he had been dirty, if he had been taking money from the drug dealer, he would have had motive to kill the drug dealer. Kill the witness and who can say what really happened?

Kill Maitland and who will say Ian Shivers murdered the federal agent? Not Ian Shivers and not a crooked cop.

Maybe the fact that it wasn't on television was a good sign. Maybe Joe Roddy, in spite of his tight-ass fed look, was a fraud. Maybe he was just another thug in the wrong place at the wrong time. Maybe it would blow over.

Maybe . . . bullshit.

Maitland lay back on the couch. The lamp and the television became a blur and he fell asleep.

He awoke at dawn. The television was not on. Sometime in the night he must have switched it off. He had used his overcoat as a blanket. He cursed himself for falling asleep down here. He sat up and put his feet on the floor. He looked around. Mrs. Cavendish was not up yet. He wondered if he should bother going upstairs and getting any more sleep. It was probably even colder up there. He had come to believe there was no place on earth colder than an English bedroom.

He decided to make some coffee instead. There was no milk in the refrigerator. Maitland remembered that they still delivered milk to the doorsteps in England. A custom he liked.

He opened the front door. There was no milk on the step. He looked left and right and that was when he stepped back in.

He closed the door and locked it.

He went to the front window and looked out the side, keeping his body hidden.

Down the street was a car that stood out. A new BMW five series, shiny and bright. Silver colored with orange and yellow stripes on the sides. Emergency colors. Blue lights on the roof.

He did not know that it was an ARV (Armed Response Vehicle), used by the CO19 division of Scotland Yard. The formal name of the unit was Specialist Firearms Command, the SWAT team of the London Metropolitan Police. Maitland did not know its formal designation. But he knew a police car when he saw one. And he knew they were here for him.

How? he thought.

He traced back his steps since getting off the plane. The Waring Hotel, the unofficial renting of the used car from the Pakistani, this forlorn bed and breakfast . . . was it his cell phone? A GPS device within? . . . he had picked up the phone after he checked in here. After he called the Waring and . . .

Shit. That was it. He had called the Waring from Mrs. Cavendish's phone. The police had checked with the Waring and traced the number back here. Stupid. Not that he would have known then that the police would be after him. But stupid nonetheless.

Maitland put his coat on. He felt his pockets. The .45 was still there. He moved to the back of the house. At the kitchen door he measured the distance between him and the garage. A tiny English garden, maybe less than fifteen yards. But if they had a man on the roof, pointing a sniper's rifle down at him . . . *fuck it, go.*

Maitland crossed the yard and went in the side door to the garage. There were two cars in the garage. The Ford Granada and Mrs. Cavendish's Geo. They might know about the Ford, but they would definitely know about Mrs. Cavendish's car. Besides, he couldn't steal Mrs. Cavendish's car. She was a good lady and she didn't deserve that. She didn't deserve to have police hammering in her front door either. He shouldn't have come to her home. He shouldn't have come to England.

The garage door was not electric. It would have to be opened manually. If there was a cop in the alley he would hear it and Maitland would be busted. *What's all this then?* . . . Arrest him and find the gun he had in his pocket . . . *Oh-ho, what have we here?* . . . shit, what a scene that would be. But he couldn't stay in this goddamn garage forever. The police were going to find him here anyway.

It was dawn and he had fallen asleep on the couch and had been lucky enough to see the police car down the street. Lucky, perhaps, but maybe it would have been better to have been upstairs asleep when the police came busting in pointing guns at him and then he wouldn't have to run anymore, wouldn't have to think, but that was a loser's way of looking at it.

Maitland got in the Ford and started it. He walked to the garage door and lifted it up. Grey light came into the garage. Maitland got back into the Ford. He made a left turn and drove slowly down the alley. The row houses crept by and soon he reached the side street.

There was another BMW police car there.

It wasn't fully blocking the exit to the street, but there wasn't space enough to go through. He saw two uniformed police officers standing by it. One of them had an H&K rifle slung over his shoulder.

Maitland felt his heart hammering. He observed the cops. One of them was holding a cigarette, his body relaxed, shooting the shit with another patrolman. They were waiting for orders. Maitland knew a cop's body language. They were waiting to hear from a superior officer. They were still setting up, still waiting. The police car was blocking egress to the street, but not fully, which meant they were waiting to move it down the alley behind Mrs. Cavendish's house. They hadn't started yet. They were waiting to engage.

Put it in reverse, jam the accelerator down. Escape.

Or, put it in first, jam the accelerator and smack the police car out of the way. Pray that the damage to the car does not disable it. Escape.

Maitland took a deep breath. They don't know about the car, he thought. Not yet. They know about the call from Mrs. Cavendish's house, but they haven't talked with the Pakistani who rented him the car and put the cash in his pocket. They don't know about the car because the transaction was not recorded. *They do not know.*

Maitland pressed the horn down.

The police officer with the rifle turned to look at him.

Maitland put an irritated, impatient look on his face and gestured a *move it* to the police car.

107

The cop looked back at him. Maitland looked back at him like he was late for work. A very long moment passed and then the cop called out to the police officer behind the wheel of the BMW. The BMW started and moved forward.

The cop waved Maitland through.

Maitland made a right turn and drove away, keeping it in second gear, keeping it slow until the police vehicle was no longer in his rearview mirror.

TWENTY

"I'll not take the responsibility," the senior man from the CO19 said.

Inspector Martin said, "You'll not? Your man lets this bloody criminal drive past and you'll not take the responsibility? He didn't even note the bleeding license number."

They were standing in front of Mrs. Cavendish's house. Mrs. Cavendish was in the house, still in her bathrobe, serving tea to plainclothes detectives and a couple of uniformed men of the CO19. The American was gone.

Mrs. Cavendish said she had not seen Evan Maitland since yesterday, but she believed she had heard him come home last night and turn the telly on downstairs. She said he was a nice bloke, a right gentleman. She said she couldn't believe he would harm anyone. She said she had allowed him to park his car in the garage in back.

The Detective Inspector and the CO19 man argued with each other and Sergeant Raines cut in, calling the CO19 man a fucking fool. The CO19 man got red in the face and said, "See here. You're the one that got us into this fucking mess. If any man of mine had escorted an American FBI agent into the lair of a known criminal without proper authorization I'd've sacked him."

There was more shouting. Inspector Martin pushed Sergeant Raines away from the CO19 man.

Inspector Martin got Raines alone and said, "Easy, Bill."

109

"Asshole," Raines said.

"He's a friend of the DCI," Martin said. "You don't want to get put on suspension."

"Fuck him."

"Bill," Martin said, "we're already in enough trouble as it is. We've got to meet with the Americans today. Treasury and FBI."

"If these fools had done their job, we'd have been able to give them Maitland. On a plate."

Martin eyed the younger sergeant. "Would you have preferred they bring him in dead or alive, Bill?"

Bill Raines looked back at his superior officer. "Makes no difference to me," Raines said.

Martin said, "I'm going inside to talk to the lady. I suggest you cool down."

Martin went in the house. Raines looked at the CO19 officers and they looked back at him, exchanging sullen expressions. Raines walked down the street and around the corner. He found a sweet shop.

There was an Indian woman behind the counter. Raines flashed her his tin and said, "I need to use your phone."

"Don't you have a mobile?" the woman said.

Christ, Raines thought. *These fucking people.* He said, "It's not working. Police business."

"Yes, sir," the Indian woman said. And directed him to a small room behind the counter. Raines went into the tiny office and closed the door behind him. He picked up the telephone on the desk and dialed a number.

Ian Shivers answered.

"It's me," Raines said. "I'm in Carshalton."

"Yes?" Ian said.

"We almost found him here. He got away."

"How?"

"I don't know. We had CO19 here. They bunged it up."

"Do you know where he is now?"

"No."

Ian sighed.

"I'm sorry, Ian. We'll find him."

"You *better* find him. And when you do, you kill him."

"Pardon?"

"You're not following me, Bill. I don't want the police to have him. I want the fucker dead. He can identify you and he can identify me."

"I . . . I'm not CO19. I'm not authorized to carry a weapon."

"I gave you a shooter six months ago. Have you lost it?"

"No. I . . . look, Ian. I can't do that."

"Listen, you ponce. You'll do what I fuckin' tell you. I'm not going to be pulled in for questioning by the coppers because Maitland says he saw me kill an American policeman."

"They're not going to believe that."

"No, they're not because they're never going to hear him say it. Do you understand me? We can't have this fellah about."

"Ian—"

"Shut up. If I go down for this, I'll have you done. Do you understand? I'll have Kenny cut your fucking face to ribbons before he stabs you in the heart. You, your wife, your kids."

"Ian—"

"You belong to us, Bill. You've made your bargain. There's no getting out now."

"Alright, Ian. Alright . . ."

Ian could hear the trembling voice of the policeman.

Ian sighed and said, "All right, Bill. Sorry for getting rough with you."

". . . it's okay."

"Sorry about making that remark about your family."

"It's all right, Ian."

"How is Margie, by the way?" Ian's voice was smooth, modulated.

Sergeant Raines closed his eyes, opened them. "She's okay, I guess."

"Good," Ian said. "Find Maitland. Find him before they do. And keep me advised. Okay?"

"Yes, sir."

Raines put the phone down. He thought of his wife and two little girls and he started to shake. He stifled a sob. He could not allow Martin to see him like this. He . . . could . . . not.

A few minutes later he was able to leave the sweet shop.

TWENTY-ONE

There were too many cameras.

Everywhere you went in central London. Security cameras, watching you. On street corners, on buildings, at bus stops. Part of Tony Blair's Big Brother society, which he called Cool Britainia. Maitland noticed the cameras when he first arrived in London but he hadn't paid much attention to it. Now it was getting to him. There was a camera mounted to a building where he was about to park his car. He saw the camera swivel on its electric mount and he kept driving and parked somewhere else. *What good does it do?* he thought. Does it actually help prevent crime? Two days ago he had watched Ian Shivers shoot a federal officer to death. Cameras inside the apartment would have helped prove that Maitland was innocent. Though they wouldn't have been much help to the agent. He saw the cameras and he thought about the cameras seeing him. *There.* There he is, the American wanted for murder. Call Ape Management. Bring him in. Stop him, arrest him, take the stolen gun away from him.

Carrying a gun was a big no-no in England. That, Maitland knew. He had read about the man in England who had shot and killed the person who broke into his home. They had sent the homeowner to prison. Some Englishmen thought that was the real crime. In the States, they probably wouldn't have even filed charges on the homeowner.

"You like guns," Bianca had once said to him. She'd probably said it more than once. Maybe there was something to it. To him, it was a tool, no worse or better than the man holding it. Guns had saved his life more than once. Saved Bianca's too, though he would never remind her of it. In any event, he was glad he had one now.

But the cameras were getting to him. He wondered if he'd lose it and use up all his ammo shooting out the cameras. He had about enough to take out about a block's worth. Was it true that reality television had started in Britain . . . ? Thanks, England.

After he parked the car, he turned up the collar of his coat and walked down a street. London covered so much ground. It was a civilized place with televisions and electricity and running water and maybe even heat in some places. But he felt trapped. He *was* trapped. If he tried to go to the airport he would be arrested. If he went to the police, they would arrest him and put him in jail and the crooked cop whose name he did not know would testify against him. If he tried to check into another hotel they would ask him for his identification and then his name might be put into some sort of data bank and the police would be notified.

He could call Jack Barrington, the diamond merchant, and ask him for his help. But he hardly knew the man. And Barrington would probably advise him to turn himself in. Or turn him in himself. More to the point, Barrington hardly knew him. Would he believe Maitland's story that he had been framed? Maitland tried to picture it turned around: a man from England coming to Chicago and a day later claiming that he had been framed by the Chicago police. Maitland may or may not believe the man was framed. But would he help him?

And these fucking cameras all over the place. Where do you hide?

Maitland went into a coffee shop on a corner. He ordered a

coffee and a Danish and found a booth. He picked up a newspaper and held it in front of his face as he tried to read it. Like a spy in a comedy.

The paper told him that Rupert Murdoch was still losing money in China and the photograph of Murdoch's very pretty, much younger Chinese wife suggested something of a correlation. Posh and Becks were still prostituting themselves in Los Angeles. The drug of choice in Manchester was no longer ecstasy but methamphetamine.

Nothing about an American treasury agent being killed.

Joe Roddy. U.S. Treasury.

The last words Roddy would say.

What was he doing here?

Why would Shivers want to kill him? Why would he be so bold as to murder an American agent? Even for a gangster with police connections, it was a high-risk move. There had to be a reason.

Maitland just a pawn in the game of life. Except it was the Shivers' game. And Maitland's life.

And a police bobby was walking into the coffee shop.

Maitland put the newspaper between him and the bobby. He peered by the side of it and saw the bobby order a cup of tea. Another police officer joined him, the second one a woman. Both of them in uniform. They talked with each other. The female cop ordered a doughnut and they walked to a booth and took a seat.

Maitland waited two minutes before he left. He walked down the street and around the corner. He was still tired, having spent an uncomfortable night on a couch, sleeping in his clothes. He was tired of running. He was tired of thinking. He was tired of being scared. He needed to rest. He checked his watch. It was a little past nine in the morning, London time. He couldn't remember what time it was in Chicago. He wondered

115

if there was a movie theater nearby. A place he could go in and find a seat and go to sleep in the dark.

But he crossed another street and there was no movie theater in sight. A police car drove past him on his left. He made a point of not looking at it, but instead slowing to a stop and looking to his right. The sign above the door said Murray House. In the window was a paper sign saying, "Scottish Independence Lecture, 9:30. The Hon. Sandy Holroyd."

Maitland walked in. A large woman greeted him at a table in a foyer. She asked if he was there for the lecture. Maitland said he was.

She said, "You're American?"

"Yes," he said. "Of Scottish descent."

"Oooh. Would you like some tea?"

"Why not?" he said. He didn't want to hurt her feelings.

She escorted him into a room holding around twenty people. Maitland took a seat near the back. The next few minutes passed as another dozen or so people waded in and took seats. A short, stout guy wearing a tweed jacket and vest took the podium. The crowd went respectfully quiet. Sandy Holroyd turned out to be a man. He said, "Let me begin by saying that although I'm a Scot, I am impartial: I don't care who beats England."

Much laughter. And Maitland thought, *Oh, no.* The tone set.

Maitland remembered an English couple buying an armoire from his antique store. The husband had no interest in furniture and left his wife alone to deal with Bianca. He and Maitland fell into a conversation that, to his surprise, Maitland had enjoyed. The Englishman had recently seen *The Patriot,* the Mel Gibson movie, and was apparently disgusted by it. He said the British soldiers portrayed in the film were little better than Nazis, and there was this nonsense discussion between Heath Ledger, playing Gibson's son, and his black slave about fighting for their freedom. The Englishman said, "Yes, in about a hundred years.

If the British had won, that slave would have been freed *then.*"
The Englishman didn't have a very high opinion of Mel Gibson.
He said *Braveheart* was absolute rubbish, filled with historical
inaccuracies. He said William Wallace was rich, not poor. That
he was spectacularly cruel and violent, even for that time. That
he had never even met Edward II's wife, let alone impregnated
her. And that he wasn't Australian.

Maitland liked that Englishman. He thought of him now and
he wondered if Mel Gibson's violent fantasy period piece had
anything to do with starting the present movement for Scottish
independence. He did know the speaker in this room was boring him and irritating him. He thought if he listened much
longer, he'd pine for the salad days of the British Empire.

The speaker droned on. Maitland folded his arms, put his
chin on his chest and went to sleep.

It was the heavyset woman who woke him.

"Are you alright, dear?"

"Yes, I'm sorry," Maitland said.

"It's alright. Would you like me to call you a taxi?"

"No," Maitland stood up, feeling a little ashamed. "It was
interesting. Really."

"Sean Connery was here last month," she said.

"Oh. Well, I'm sure that was nice."

The woman smiled at him. Maitland saw himself out.

There were no police officers near his car. Maitland got in it
and drove away. He felt a little better now.

The lecture brought back a memory. Community college in
suburban Chicago. There was a history course he had hated, the
teacher a Korean War veteran who had never really healed.
Once the man had cried in front of the class. Maitland thought
the guy was okay, but felt sorry for him. It was a gut course
anyway. Like the other students, Maitland learned little about

117

20th century American history but a lot about the poor instructor's life. Maitland took to skipping the class to avoid the social discomfort and instead would use that hour to take a nap in the college library. There was a private reading room in the back of that library with a very nice couch. He liked that place.

It was too bad there wasn't a couch in another room near the Scottish Independence lecture hall. He could have gotten more rest.

Library.

Maitland pulled over at the next shop he saw. He went inside and asked for a telephone book. He found an address and asked for directions.

The library was in Islington. A small branch about the size of a neighborhood bank. He sat in front of a personal computer and punched Julian Atherton's name into the Google website. He found something in the *Daily Sun*. Atherton was pictured with a very pretty blond woman who was, apparently, a celebrity in England but virtually unknown in America. They were at a horse race in Brighton. The photo caption said Atherton was a businessman and the owner of a rugby team called the Watney Street Bulldogs.

Not much else on Atherton.

Maitland sat for a moment. Then he went back to Google and typed in Watney Street Bulldogs.

There was more information on the rugby team than the man. The sports page of another newspaper's website said there was a match at two o'clock this afternoon.

TWENTY-TWO

The stands were about the size of an American high school football stadium, though the field looked smaller. On one side of the field were bleachers surrounded by a brick wall base, on the other side there was no brick wall base, just stands. Perhaps for the visiting fans.

It was cold and slightly foggy and the stands were densely populated and it was not all that easy to see the players on the field. It took Maitland a while to figure out that one team was wearing dark green jerseys and the other was wearing crimson. Britain in winter was a sort of black and white film. The players seemed muddy and beat up. Maitland tried to get into the game but couldn't follow it. There were no long passes, no plays. It just seemed like a bunch of large, burly guys groaning and shoving each other with sporadic attempts of someone breaking away and running down the field.

After one guy was tackled and brought to the ground, Maitland could have sworn he saw two players on the opposing team kick him. *Gentleman's game, my ass.*

Maitland wondered about England and about what sort of preconceptions he had formed before coming here. It was not that he had expected it to be a land of men in bowler hats carrying umbrellas, Henry Higgins and Hugh Grant types charming the ladies with an affected stammer . . . well, maybe he had thought that. Nevertheless, he had not expected to encounter brutes like Ian and Ken Shivers let alone see men on the ground getting kicked in the ribs.

Before he left, he had discussed England with Bianca. Bianca was a funny lady. She deplored racism in the United States and more than once had lectured Maitland about U.S. historical mistreatment of blacks, as if he had had a hand in it. Yet bring up the subject of Europe and she didn't hesitate to stereotype anyone. At different times, she had told him that the French were rude assholes, the Eastern Europeans coarse and vulgar, the Germans bullheaded and pushy, the Belgians boring, and so forth.

Maitland asked her, "What about Italians?"

"Criminals," she said. "Every one of them."

Bianca said the English were just hooligans. She said you could go to any resort in Malta or Spain or Greece and always, *always*, it was the English tourists that were the biggest trouble. Consistently, the Brits abroad would get blind drunk, start fights, and piss in the streets. Bianca said that when the World Cup was in Germany, everybody was afraid of the English football fans and the Germans looked civil by comparison. Something she hadn't thought was possible.

Maitland scanned the opposite side of the field. He found Julian Atherton on what would be called the fifty-yard line in the States. Next to him was a dark-haired woman wearing a fur coat and a wool hat. Maitland looked around Atherton. He did not see any of the men who had tried to kill him. He did not see any bodyguards.

Would Atherton leave himself exposed like this? Maybe the dark-haired woman had an Uzi under her fur.

Maitland walked over to the other side of the field. He took a seat twelve rows behind Atherton, not close enough to hear what he was saying, but close enough to see the body language between him and the woman. The match ended and the woman kissed him on the cheek and they went their separate ways.

Keeping crowds between them, Maitland followed Atherton to an enclosed hall beneath the stands. The hall was filled with people. There was a bar at the back with a maternal-looking woman serving pints of beer. The tables and chairs were cheap and functional, an atmosphere not unlike that of a church's parish hall. The rugby players mixed with the fans, who paid small dues to be members of the club.

Everyone there was white. Rough-looking men and heavy-set girls and even a few kids running around. A man at a table said to his friends, "What do you throw a Paki who's drowning? His wife and kids." This got a big laugh.

Maitland went to the bar and bought a pint. He kept his back to Julian Atherton, who was sitting at a table with two rugby players and a fourth man wearing an expensive suit. Maitland thought, *You can leave now. But where would you go?*

He walked over to Atherton's table.

Atherton looked up at him, his eyes widening.

"Hello, Julian," Maitland said.

Atherton said, "What are you doing here?"

"We never finished our discussion the other night."

Atherton smiled. Maitland held onto his glass. The men at the table seemed confused.

"Clever," Atherton said. "Gentlemen, would you excuse us for a moment?"

The men left, one of the rugby players hesitating for a moment, giving Maitland a threatening stare.

Maitland sat down.

Julian Atherton said, "What do you want?"

"An explanation," Maitland said.

Atherton shook his head, as if dealing with a child. "It's out of my hands," he said.

"You set me up," Maitland said.

Atherton waved his hand dismissively. He said, "A misunderstanding. Why don't you discuss it with Ian?"

"Why don't we discuss it with the police? Both of us. Get this cleared up."

"Why should I?" Atherton said. "I wasn't there."

Moments passed. Maitland had the .45 with him. But what was he supposed to do? Shoot this fucker for taunting him? Gun down a smarmy asshole for revenge, go to jail for murder . . . look at the man now, pleased with himself.

Atherton smiled again.

And Maitland found himself trembling with rage. His hand moving to the gun in his coat pocket, wondering if it would be worth a life sentence just to blow the smile off this man's face.

Maitland said, "Why?"

"You were in the right place at the right time."

"That's not good enough," Maitland said and reached across the table and grabbed Julian Atherton by the lapels and jerked him out of his chair. It knocked the drinks off the table. Julian was on his feet and Maitland punched him in the kidneys. Julian gasped, his ability to speak temporarily disabled.

"Come on," Maitland said. "We're going to the police, get this straightened out."

Shit, it was a risk. Among a crowd of hostiles, a good many of them burly rugby players. The thing was to get out fast. Maitland moved quickly, pulling Atherton along with him. A woman asked what was wrong and Maitland said, "He's not feeling well. We're going to go outside and get some air."

The rugby player who had given the hard look moved in front of him. Maitland took the .45 out of his pocket and prodded the barrel against the man's belly.

The man looked down at the gun. "Christ," he said, suddenly frightened.

"Yeah," Maitland said. "Back off."

He got Atherton out the door and halfway to his car when he

122

saw the red Jaguar MKII coming down the street. There was clear plastic where the window had been busted out. Behind the wheel of the Jaguar was Cliff Wilkinson. Next to him a dark-haired man Maitland hadn't seen before, another man in the back.

The Jag screeched to a halt. A stocky man got out of the back holding a short barreled Mac-10 machine gun. The dark-haired man had a Glock.

Cliff Wilkinson got out of the car and yelled to both of them, "Don't shoot the fixer."

Maitland held Atherton in front of him.

Cliff Wilkinson approached them, a broad smile on his face. He said, "Where you going, sunshine?"

Maitland pulled out the .45. "That's close enough," he said.

"Oh, got a shooter, do you?"

"Don't shoot me!" Atherton said. "For Christ's sake, don't shoot me!"

"Shut up," Wilkinson said.

A moment passed, none of the men saying anything. Their breaths fogging in the cold.

Maitland said, "This man's my prisoner."

"Where you going to take him?" Wilkinson said, the smile still on his face.

"The police."

Cliff Wilkinson said, "Law's not exactly on your side, guv-nor."

Maitland said, "I'll take my chances."

The stocky man was circling around Maitland's left, holding the Mac-10 up. And now Maitland saw that Wilkinson had a pistol at his side too.

Maitland said to Cliff Wilkinson, "That man gets any closer, I'll kill him, then you."

"Will you now?" Wilkinson said. And Maitland thought, *He's got nerve. A lot of it.* Wilkinson's voice was calm, like he was confident that he was in control of the situation. And Maitland was beginning to think he was. Maitland knew he was losing it. They didn't want to shoot Atherton, but there were three of them, all armed, circling him now . . .

A truck was approaching. A medium-size truck, tall and long enough and it had to move to the right of the road to avoid hitting the Jaguar. The men looked over at it and Maitland shoved Atherton forward into Wilkinson and ran in front of the truck, cutting it close but getting past it, and then the truck was between him and the men with guns and Maitland ran down the street and around the corner.

There were cars parked on both sides of this street. Maitland ran, turning around once to see all three men pursuing him, the one with the Glock pistol in front, now pointing it and taking a shot. It didn't connect, the guy was running and not stopping to get a steady shooting stance the way a professional or a cop would and he was a good fifty yards behind Maitland.

Maitland moved right and got between two parked vehicles, a van in front of him, a car behind. He stood behind the van. He was right handed and that was why he had gone right. He would be able to shield himself behind the van, exposing only part of his body if he took a shot.

Using two hands he held the .45 up. The guy with the Glock saw him, kept running, lifted his Glock and fired. *Stupid,* Maitland thought, and shot him twice in the chest. The man flipped up as if he had run into a clothesline and fell on his back.

The man with the machine gun went to his right and took cover behind a car. Cliff Wilkinson ran to the other side of the street and dodged behind an SUV.

The stocky man with the Mac-10 crouched behind a car. He

looked across the street to find Cliff, but Cliff had dodged behind another vehicle. The American had put down Derek, who was lying in the street. The stocky man knew the American was hiding behind the blue van. But the American only had a pistol, which was no match for a machine gun. The blue van was a small panel vehicle with windows at the driver and passenger seats and at the back, but no windows on the sides. It would help the American hide. The Mac-10 had nine-millimeter rounds, but would they go through the front window of the blue van and out the back windows and fill the American with holes? The stocky man peered over the back of the car. The front window of the blue van was in sight. He raised higher and now he could see out the back windows of the van. No one there. The American was crouched down. Maybe the American was looking across the street for Cliff. Maybe the American didn't know that he—the stocky man—was here too.

The stocky man crept out from behind the car. Between him and the blue van were three cars. On his right a row of houses. The stocky man looked at the windows of the houses to see if his reflection would be visible to the American crouched behind the van. It was not—the windows were too high. The stocky man began moving toward the blue van. He kept his steps quiet, his body low, the machine gun in front of him, his finger on the trigger. He passed the second car and then the third and then he was at the blue van. He put himself against the van, breathed for a moment. Then he moved forward, creeping silently. The corner of the van coming close now . . .

He swung around the corner and pulled the trigger. The machine gun let out a burst . . . at nothing.

There was no one there.

The stocky man stepped behind the blue van. He looked into the back windows. And that was when he heard the shot and felt his ankle explode.

The stocky man cried out as he fell to the ground, dropping the machine gun.

The stocky man turned and looked at the car parked behind the blue van. Lying under the car, on his stomach, was the American pointing a .45 at his face.

The machine gun was about a foot from the stocky man's hand. All he would have to do was reach for it . . .

The American shook his head and said, "You don't want to do that."

From across the street, Cliff called out to him. Cliff was still taking cover behind an SUV.

"Marko!"

In a low voice, Maitland said, "Tell him where I am and you die."

The stocky man breathed heavily. He wondered if his foot was still connected to his leg. He wondered if he would go into shock. He wondered if he should feel lucky he wasn't lying dead in the street like Derek.

"*Marko!*" Fear in Cliff Wilkinson's voice.

The stocky man breathed in and out, twice. Then he said in a tone above a whisper, "What—what do—you—want me to do?"

"Curl up," Maitland said. "Like a baby sleeping, your hands between your legs. Then roll over so your back is toward me." Maitland added, "Do it *slowly.*"

The stocky man did as he was told, holding his mouth tight to avoid letting out a cry. He made the mistake, once, of trying to use the leg that had been shot.

"*Marko! What's going on?*"

Maitland got out from under the car. He stayed crouched behind it. Maitland looked at the crouched figure trembling a few feet away from him. The machine gun lay on the ground.

Maitland said, "If I were you, I'd hope my friend is more interested in getting you to a hospital than coming after me."

The stocky man didn't answer.

Maitland said, "Count to a hundred before you move or call out to him. Remember, I could easily put a bullet in your back."

The stocky man said, "I can't move."

"Whose fault is that?" Maitland said.

Sirens in the distance. Getting closer now.

Maitland moved down the row of cars, crouching so as not to be seen from the street. He did not see the third man. He had a feeling the third man wasn't so tough when he knew two of his friends had been taken out of the picture. It was a one-armed man against another now and bullies generally don't savor a fair fight.

But now he had the police to worry about. He would have welcomed the sight of them earlier when he had Atherton with him. But now Atherton was gone and even if he wasn't, he would side with the two gunmen.

Maitland got off the street and around a corner and now he could see a police vehicle about three blocks away. Another one of those goddamn flashy-painted BMWs, which meant there were armed police officers inside.

Maitland put the .45 in his coat pocket. He maintained a steady walk, looking ahead. The police car coming fast, buzzing angrily. You couldn't have a gunfight in a residential neighborhood and not have someone call the police. He hoped the police would be fully occupied with the three armed men around the corner. But he was walking in the same direction the police car was approaching and it probably wasn't the only vehicle coming to the scene. *Walk, don't run,* Maitland thought. *If they see you running, they'll chase and then where will you be?*

Up ahead, about thirty yards, was an Underground sign, stairs descending below the street. He walked toward the steps, going neither fast nor slow. The police car was about fifty yards away from him when he reached the stairs and walked down.

He heard the police car zoom by.

He increased his pace, moving quickly down the steps. The stairs turned ninety degrees and he moved quicker. And then he heard it. Up on the street, the screech of tires, the unusual whirring sound of an automobile being driven in reverse.

Shit.

Maitland took the gun out of his coat pocket and slipped it into his sport jacket pocket. He went through the ticket counter. Then he reached the train platform. There were no more than a dozen people there and that was bad. Maitland looked around, but kept moving. He took his tan overcoat off and held it over his arm. He walked to a trash bin and stuffed the overcoat inside. Then he walked to the edge of the platform. No train. People were quieter than they would be on the New York subway. He wished it were louder. He wished there were riff-raff around, people causing a distraction. He wished there were more people. He wished the fucking train would get here.

Then he heard the *woosh* and the blare of a horn and a woman nearby sighed as if to say, *about time.* And Maitland couldn't agree more, though he was not aware of how long the woman had been standing there.

Maitland turned to the woman and said, "Is the train late?"

The woman was in her mid to late twenties. She had black curly hair and a buxom figure. Black mini-skirt and black leggings, red sweater under a hip-length coat. She looked at Maitland like he was slow or something. She said, "Late? Did you not hear the announcement?"

The train slowed, the brakes' screech echoing in the tunnel.

"No," Maitland said.

"Lucky you are," the woman said. "Bleeding signal failures. It was due half hour ago."

"Oh."

The train rolled to a stop. Maitland walked alongside the woman to the door. Approximately fifty yards away, a uniformed police officer walked out to the platform.

The woman said to Maitland, "Last week, it was 'non-arrival of staff.' It's always something."

A cockney accent. The *a* in late, the faint *f* in something.

"Well," Maitland said, "what are you going to do?" Now he saw that the uniformed police officer was joined by a plain-clothes cop wearing a blue overcoat. They had serious, hunter looks on their faces.

There was an available seat nearby. Maitland gestured to it and the woman said, "You sure?"

"Please."

"Thanks, mate." She sat down. Maitland took hold of a pole and faced her, his back to the windows facing the platform. The policemen were walking down the platform now, looking in.

The young lady looked at him, a little surprised at his forwardness, but not seeming put off. She said, "You visiting from the States?"

The doors closed. The train started moving.

There was no point in trying to persuade he was British. "Yeah," he said. "I'm from California."

"Well, aren't you a gentleman, giving a lady a seat."

"You're a pretty lady."

The woman smiled. "Cheeky," she said. "You shouldn't waste your time, though, chatting me up. I've got a boyfriend."

The train was going fast now, the outside a blur. Maitland relaxed, a little. He was trembling inside, the fears coming to the surface. Safe for now. Maybe . . .

The woman said, "Did you hear what I said?"

"Pardon?"

The woman looked at him now, her expression concerned. She said, "You all right?"

I've just killed a man and the police are after me. And I'm in a foreign country that I can't leave.

"I'm fine," Maitland said. "Sorry. It was nice talking to you."

He walked away from her. She watched him go into the next car.

TWENTY-THREE

He waited two stops before he got off the train. Then he got on
another train. He didn't remember how long he stayed on that
one. He got off and walked up the steps into daylight. He was
on another street in London on another cold, gray day. Apart
from that, he didn't know where he was. He missed the car.
Having it wouldn't solve his problems. But he believed he would
feel better if he had it. Maybe if he did he'd drive it to Scotland
and try to see if he could find a way off this island there. But he
knew it wouldn't do any good. He was stuck in this place. Two
men dead now, one of them a treasury agent, the other a piece
of shit who had it coming. But what difference did it make? He
was pegged now. Profiled. Violent American carrying a gun.

He took the phone out of his jacket pocket. There was a message. He checked it and heard a friendly voice.

"Evan, this is Sophie Palmer. I might be able to help you.
Call me back."

She must have called while he was underground. She was a
nice lady, being helpful. She didn't deserve to be mixed up with
him. But he didn't know what else to do. He was cold and
lonely and lost.

He called her back.

Hellos were exchanged and then she said, "Any luck?"

"Oh . . . not much," he said, suppressing a bitter laugh. "How
about you?"

"I might have something. Do you have a minute?"

"Yes. Would you mind if we met?"

"Well . . . I had plans actually. A dinner date."

"Oh." Maitland could see that it was already getting dark. The place had less winter light than Chicago. He said, "Well, can you cancel it?"

Silence on the other end.

Maitland said, "I'm sorry, but I don't have long to stay in London. I can buy you dinner."

He heard a sigh. "That's not the point," Sophie said. "It would be rude. What you're asking is . . ."

"I know," Maitland said. "I just thought that—I'd just like to see you again."

Another pause.

"I don't know . . ."

"It would mean something to me," Maitland said, which wasn't a complete lie.

Sophie said, "All right. There's a place called the Millburgh Thistle. That's in Islington. Meet you in an hour?"

Maitland suppressed a laugh of relief. "Great," he said. "I'll see you then."

Forty-five minutes later a cab deposited him there.

The Millburgh Thistle had an upstairs and a downstairs. Both floors had a bar. The bar downstairs was big and long and there were two flat screen televisions behind it. There was another big screen television on the wall in the dining area. It reminded Maitland too much of an American sports bar. Except instead of football and basketball on the screens, it was soccer. There were fans inside the bar, many of them wearing team colors and scarves. Their chatter was unmistakably British, more pointed and literate and existential than the Americans. Things like:

". . . You're a disgrace, Rooney. A disgrace . . ."

132

". . . Well saved, Percy."

"Rubbish!"

"This is appalling . . ."

"What a sad, shabby performance."

And so forth.

Maitland came in from the cold and took a seat at the downstairs bar. The bartender asked what he'd like and Maitland said Scotch on the rocks, no water. The bartender brought back a glass of Scotch with a couple of ice cubes no bigger than your thumb. Maitland shook his head and drank it anyway.

Maitland had never been much of a drinker, but the glass was drained before Sophie Palmer arrived. The shakes had left him when she touched him on the elbow and said hello.

"Hey," Maitland said.

Sophie Palmer wore jeans and a brown sweater with a white collar sticking out. A plaid scarf around her neck and an overcoat. She put her gloves in her pockets.

"Hello." She said, "Ooh, you're all cold. Did you lose your coat?"

"Yeah, sort of," Maitland said. "Can I buy you a drink?"

"Not here. It's too loud. Let's go upstairs."

It was quieter upstairs. The bar was small and there was no television. There was a fireplace with a fire. There were tables and there were booths. The booths were cherry wood and they had backs high enough to hide the occupants from a distance.

It was Sophie who suggested they sit at a booth.

She took off her coat but left her scarf around her neck. Maitland left his jacket on. He still hadn't warmed up.

He noticed Sophie looking at him after they gave their drink orders to the waitress. Maybe it was because she was concerned. Maybe now that she was seeing him, she was wondering if he was all that glad to see her. Maybe she was seeing more desperation than romantic interest. Maybe she was seeing that he was scared.

Maitland gave her a weak smile. "So, what did you find out for me?"

Sophie said, "You mean the chair?"

"Yes."

"I found out that it was sold at an auction in New York in 1986 to an investment banker. Or rather, his wife. Rather interesting, in fact. The fellow who purchased it got in trouble with the Securities and Exchange Commission for some sort of fraud. Had to pay a large fine and, I believe, file bankruptcy."

"And the chair went to the bankruptcy trustee?"

"No. The chair disappeared."

"What?"

"Someone unloaded it, the mister or the missus. Hid the sale from the trustee. Or maybe it was sold before the law came after them."

"Where are they now?"

"Busted up. The husband, he went to California and died in an auto accident. No, wait. Actually, it was a motorbike. Apparently, he was riding down one of those twisty canyon roads in Malibu and went headlong into a car. Smashed him like a bug."

"How do you know this?"

"How do I know about his death?"

"Yeah."

"That was on the Internet. Write-up in the *Wall Street Journal*, I believe, in the *Financial Times* as well. The auction information was not Internet accessible." She smiled. "So it wasn't a complete waste of time, asking for my help."

"Is the wife alive?"

"That I don't know. I couldn't find her."

Maitland sighed. "Well, that's great. I'd've been better off looking in New York."

"Well, I don't see how," Sophie said. "I never said the chair was still in New York. You still believe it's here, don't you?"

The waiter returned with their drinks. He asked if they had decided on a meal. Sophie ordered a steak sandwich and chips. Maitland ordered chicken soup and a side of bread.

The waiter left and Sophie put her glass up. Maitland touched his glass to hers.

"Cheers," Sophie said.

"Cheers."

Sophie looked at him again, the concern returning. "Hey," she said, "you're not sorry you came, are you?"

Maitland stared at her briefly. Then he laughed. "Christ," he said, "if you only knew."

The woman studied him for a moment. An American before her, not making eye contact, looking at the table.

Sophie said, "I'm not unhappy to see you. But I could have told you all I know over the phone."

"I know that."

"Then why did you ask to see me?"

Maitland forced himself to look into her eyes. He couldn't lie to her anymore.

"Because I'm in trouble," he said.

He told her all of it. Watched her wince as he told her about the American treasury agent being killed, watched her jaw go slack as he told her about the police surrounding the bed and breakfast, watched her stare at him when he told her about shooting the man in the street.

The waiter took away their dinner plates.

Maitland said, "You don't believe me."

Sophie said, "I didn't say that."

"It's alright. I wouldn't believe me if I were you."

"I didn't say I didn't believe you. You've given names that are

135

not unfamiliar. The Shivers brothers."

"You know of them?"

"Most of London knows about them. They're famous."

"Famous? They've framed me for a murder."

"You've told me that."

"Yes, I've told you. If you don't believe me, I want you to tell me. If you don't believe me, I'll leave you alone."

"Why?"

"Because if I were you and I didn't believe me, I'd call the police. Either I'm crazy or I'm guilty."

"You left something out," Sophie said.

"Oh. You mean that I'm telling the truth?"

"Yes. Are you?"

"Yes. I'm telling you the truth."

"Why did you call me? I don't even know you."

"You're the only one I know in London."

"What about Mr. Barrington?"

Maitland didn't have an answer for that. He had thought about it earlier, but told himself he didn't want to get Barrington dragged into this. Maybe that was it. Or maybe it was a fear that Barrington wouldn't believe him and would call his friends at Scotland Yard and turn Maitland in.

"Well?" Sophie said. "What about Barrington? Why didn't you call him?"

"I don't know," Maitland said. "You called and I returned your call and . . . I'm sorry, I don't have an answer."

"You have to speak to a lawyer. You must."

"I have. My lawyer in Chicago."

"What the hell good would that do? You need someone here."

"And tell him what? What I told you? Didn't you hear what I said earlier? There's a corrupt policeman involved. He's in this. But the funny thing is, I'm not even really worried about him. I'm worried about the Shivers and their crew. They've sort of prioritized things."

"And now you've killed one of their men."

"Yeah." Maitland looked at her. The woman leaning forward, her hands clasped beneath her mouth. Her eyes soft, yet penetrating.

"I'm sorry," Maitland said.

"For what?"

"For misleading you."

"When did you do that?"

"When I called you earlier, I said I wanted to see you again and I asked you to cancel your date."

"I see. So you're not in love with me, then?"

"Like you said, I hardly know you."

"What did you want then?"

"I guess I wanted to talk to someone. I guess I didn't want to feel alone."

"How flattering."

"You know what I mean. In normal circumstances, I'd—well, who knows?"

"Yes. Who knows," Sophie said. She shook her head. "You look bloody awful."

"I'm tired."

"Where will you go now? You can't check into a hotel."

"I don't know. There are places to hide. Until this settles down." Maitland regarded the woman and said, "Listen, I'm not asking—"

"The hell you're not." Sophie leaned back and said, "Suppose I did let you stay at my place. Just for the night. How do you know I wouldn't turn you in after you fall asleep?"

"I don't, I guess. How do you know it'd be safe to let me stay?"

"I don't. I think I don't . . . I don't know." She turned away from him.

137

"Just for a few hours," Maitland said. "I have to rest. I have to sleep. I've got . . . I've got no place else."

Sophie shook her head. "I'm not even sure I like you," she said.

Maitland signaled the waiter for the check. He said, "We'll muddle through somehow." He was very tired.

TWENTY-FOUR

Kenny hit the 20 slice on the dartboard using a throwing knife instead of a dart. The knife vibrated with the impact.

Kenny said, "Where would he get a shooter? From the old woman's house?"

"I dunno," Cliff Wilkinson said.

"You don't know," Kenny said. He shook his head in a way that made Wilkinson afraid.

Ian said, "And you don't know where Marko is either?"

"I presume they took him to a hospital," Wilkinson said.

"You presume," Ian said. "Why didn't you take him yourself? Get him out of there."

"There wasn't time," Wilkinson. "Cops was coming."

Kenny said, "That's just bloody marvelous, that is."

They were in the game room at Ian's house. Kenny throwing his knife at the dartboard, ruining it, Ian sitting in a red leather chair, Cliff Wilkinson on the carpet.

Wilkinson said, "Look, he didn't get away with Julian. We've got him here now."

Ian said, "And what if you'd come later? He would have gotten away with him. We need Julian, Cliff. You know that."

"Right, Ian. But Maitland didn't know."

Ian said, "Maybe he didn't. But maybe he did. Seems this fellah's full of surprises."

"He got lucky," Wilkinson said.

Kenny said, "He killed one of our men and crippled the other.

I wouldn't call that lucky."

Ian said, "Never mind, Cliff. Go see if Julian wants a cheese sandwich or something."

Cliff walked out of the room.

Kenny said, "I expect Julian's not happy, having to bunk here."

Ian said, "Julian can leave after we meet with DeGiusti and he forges the certificates. We can't risk having the American find him again. Without our fixer, the securities might as well be toilet paper."

Kenny said, "Wonder how he found him."

"I don't know."

"He's going to suffer when I find *him*. I promise you that."

"Kenny, don't go off course. We've got to deal with these securities first."

Kenny regarded his brother. Ian. *Look at him, sitting in his red leather chair like he's Alistair Cooke hosting* Masterpiece Theater. More and more, Ian was trying to become upper class. A bloody waste of time. They were what they were and who should be ashamed of it?

Kenny said, "Didn't you tell me earlier you were worried about the police getting to him before we do?"

"Never mind what I said. He's not going to mess up this deal."

"You're not looking at the larger picture, Ian. He took out two of our boys. That's going to make headlines in what they call the criminal underworld. And then our reputation suffers. That's more important than money."

"Nothing's more important than money."

"Wrong. We make money because people fear us. They're terrified of us. A man comes into town and kills one of our men, what are we then?"

A moment passed. Then Ian said, "Vulnerable."

"Now you're twigging it," Kenny said.

TWENTY-FIVE

Maitland looked at a photo of Sophie at the park with a little boy in a school uniform. He asked, "Is this your boy?"

"Yes. He's on holiday with his dad."

Maitland said. "Switzerland, right?"

"Right," Sophie said. "Would you like a cup of tea?"

Maitland sat on the couch. "Sure."

It was a two-bedroom apartment. Clean and compact, efficient and well decorated. Maitland said, "You have a nice place."

From the kitchen, Sophie said, "You wouldn't believe how much it costs. London has gotten so expensive."

"Yeah?"

"Oh, yes. Thirty, forty years ago, you could rent a flat near Trafalgar Square for about a hundred quid a month. Walk to the pubs and the nightclubs. It's all changed now. . . . Sorry, I guess I've already told you this."

Maitland took his sport jacket off. It was chilly in here too. Maitland said, "That's all right."

Sophie said, "Margaret Thatcher's the culprit. Or hero, depending on your point of view. I don't know. When I was a little girl, the economy was terrible. The coal miners would strike and we'd have no power, sometimes for three days a week. We'd sit in the house in darkness. As late as the fifties there was still food rationing. My mum and dad used to talk about it. They didn't complain, but told me and my brother how it was.

To remind us, I suppose, how fortunate we were."

Sophie couldn't see Maitland from the kitchen. She wondered if he was still listening to her. Then she decided it didn't matter. She was aware that she was talking too much to cover up her nervousness. She could admit that to herself, admit that she was nervous. She wondered if she should be afraid.

She heard Maitland say, "Remind you of what?"

"How much better off we were. We may not have had heat or electricity a few days a month, but we weren't going hungry. . . . It's better now . . . but I don't know. I miss the old times."

From the living room, a grunt.

Sophie said, "Not that I'm worried about money myself. We're doing fine, Davy and me. David, that's my boy. But I miss the old days, in a way. We had such low expectations, but we were happy. There's no happier people than the English, you know."

Sophie set two white cups on a tray then poured tea into the cups. She said, "Do you take anything in your tea, Evan?"

She felt funny using his first name. A stranger. Perhaps a fugitive or even a lunatic. She had allowed him into her home. . . . Maybe she was the lunatic.

"Evan?"

She peered around the corner.

He was asleep on the couch. His sport coat was over his chest, a cushion over his eyes.

"Christ," Sophie said. "Insane." She got a blanket from her bedroom closet and placed it over him. Then she took a seat in her chair and sipped her tea.

She was still in the chair an hour later, smoking a cigarette, watching the man sleep. She checked her watch and saw that it was late. David, her son, would be in bed by now. Unless Malcolm, her ex-husband and David's father, had allowed him to stay up past his bedtime. She and Malcolm had been divorced for three months now, though they had been legally separated for over a year. It was over a year ago that she had found the photographs in his desk. The photographs of a naked girl. The girl's name turned out to be Joanna. She was twenty-six and she was Malcolm's legal secretary.

Sophie wondered what would have happened if she hadn't found the photos. She had not meant to find them. She had been looking for a pair of scissors. That was what she truthfully told Malcolm after she asked him about it. His first reaction was to ask her what she had been doing mucking about in his desk. Putting it on her, the bastard. But she put it back on him where it should be, and soon came the tears. Malcolm's tears, as he confessed that he was in love with the girl.

Sophie was dumbfounded. If she hadn't found the evidence, she would not have thought Malcolm capable. He had never been a womanizer. She had considered him a stable chap. Earnest and family oriented. Indeed, she was even willing to work at holding the marriage together. For David's sake and maybe even for Malcolm's. Her mum had once told her, "You've to watch em' when then they turn forty." And Malcolm was forty-one. Still, Sophie was willing to save the marriage and willing to forgive Malcolm. But Malcolm wasn't interested. He said he was in love with Joanna and wanted to marry her.

Sophie did not consider herself a vain woman. But she could not understand why Malcolm would want to marry his legal secretary. She was overweight, not very attractive, and not especially warm. Plus she wasn't very bright or even interesting. She *was* twelve years younger than Sophie, but Sophie didn't believe her youth could make up for all her deficiencies.

Malcolm had said, "You don't understand. She needs me."

"We need you too," Sophie said.

She did not beg. She did not give herself to him sexually; she would not share a husband with another woman. But she did try to persuade him to stay with his family. But he didn't want to be persuaded. Near the end, she started to think he had wanted her to find the photos.

So it was done. Her husband had left her for a younger woman. *What a cliché,* she thought.

Her girlfriends told her she should be relieved. Malcolm was a dull old sod anyway. Besides, you would never be able to trust him again.

And that part was true. She knew she never would be able to trust him again. He had acted like a boy all throughout. But Sophie wasn't sure that trust mattered to her where Malcolm was concerned. She wanted David to be in the house with Malcolm. She wanted her son to have his mummy and daddy. In time, maybe she and Malcolm could repair their relationship, rebuild trust. If they did not . . . well, they were English, weren't they? Better not to expect too much.

She had dated only three men since the break-up of the marriage. All of them dreadful. One of them asked her to spank his bum. This, on their first date. The other spent most of dinner speaking fondly of his male Latin teacher at Eton and Sophie soon gathered that he was still in love with him. Yet another kept talking about who had "the best tits in England." He was in his late forties.

Deviance, latent homosexuality, laddie boy sexism. It wasn't easy for a single girl in England. Sophie sometimes wondered if all the adolescent sexual culture in Britain wasn't a sort of cover for a national discomfort with healthy sex. She'd read Maugham's autobiography in college and remembered where he had said the English were basically not a romantic race. Englishmen were passionate about their football teams and their schools and even their country, but not their women.

She had not lied when she told Maitland she had a date

tonight. She did have one. A blind one; a friend of a friend. She had talked with him on the phone and had been unenthused, but agreed to meet him for dinner anyway. The truth was, she had nothing better to do. Until this American fugitive asked her to cancel, not knowing she would be relieved to do it.

Sophie smiled to herself. You don't trust your ex-husband, but you trust a complete stranger. And a foreign one at that. How do you explain that, Mrs. Palmer?

She doubted she could, if anyone were to ask. Perhaps it was because Evan Maitland reminded her of her brother Tom. Apart from her son, she had probably never loved anyone more than she had loved Tom. He had been a big boy, strong and athletic. A gentle giant. They had gone to the same Catholic elementary school. One day, an older boy pushed her and she fell in the mud and ruined her school dress. Tom was there in a flash and he picked up the other boy and threw him down and pushed his face in the mud. But the most courageous thing was what Tom did afterward. He escorted Sophie to the principal's office and requested that the principal telephone their mum to bring a clean uniform to the school. British schoolmasters are not used to taking requests from ten-year-old boys. The schoolmaster told Tom to get out of his office and take his little sister with him. When Tom refused until the phone call was made, the schoolmaster gave him five swats with a cricket bat. Tom took the swats without making a sound. After it was done, Tom said, "Right. Now will you make the call?" And got six more.

When he died, she wept for weeks. He was a good man and a good soldier and he would have made a good policeman. Had he lived, maybe he would have taken on the London scourge that was the Shivers brothers.

The American would not replace her brother. Nor would he replace her husband. He was a stranger and he was in trouble. Perhaps she was a fool for helping him. Perhaps he would wait for her to go to sleep and he would creep into her bedroom and attack her. Which might even be nice, that. . . . It had been so long. . . . But she could lock her bedroom door and put a chair against it if she were truly worried about that.

But maybe this was all flattering self-delusion. Maybe the American fancied younger, chubby women as well.

Maitland awoke between four and five in the morning. It took him a moment to get his bearings. He realized he was not at the bed and breakfast but at Sophie Palmer's apartment. The pretty blond woman with the ruddy cheeks and the beautiful little overbite. He let his eyes adjust to the darkness. There was a blanket over him. She must have put it there. God . . . where was she now? Maybe she was at a police station, giving his description. *Insane, criminal, liar* . . . or maybe she was in her bedroom with a chest of drawers shoved against the door. Shit. She didn't deserve this. He should not have imposed on her like this. He should have gone to the American Embassy and explained himself, but if he had done that they would have almost certainly nodded their heads and turned him over to the British police and said, what country did he think he was in, Turkey? He was suspected of killing an American federal agent.

It disturbed him that the woman had put a blanket over him. She had not even checked his jacket and taken his gun from it. She trusted him. And he had done nothing for her, nothing except mislead her into thinking he had a romantic interest in her so he could find a place to hole up from gangsters and crooked cops and cops that weren't crooked. He didn't deserve her trust and she didn't deserve to have to deal with him but it was cold outside and he didn't know where else to go and he needed a friend.

Decisions are easier when you don't have much choice. He could lie awake in the dark and stare at the ceiling and wallow in guilt and self-recrimination, but it was all a lot of navel-gazing horseshit because he knew he wouldn't leave this safe, warm place, knew he would continue to take advantage of this decent, compassionate stranger because he didn't have any other alternatives. At least, not until morning. He was too tired to think about it now. Too exhausted to move. He closed his eyes and went back to sleep.

Sophie awoke at eight A.M. when her alarm went off. She got out of bed. She was wearing underwear and a T-shirt. She looked at her bedroom door, which was locked. Last night, she had lay in bed after she turned out the light and glanced at the door and wondered if Maitland would attempt to come in. Somehow, she knew he would not. Yet she knew that anyone on the outside would say she was insane not to have locked the door. Insane indeed to have allowed him into her flat. If he was telling the truth, he was in trouble with the law and capable of violence. If he was not telling the truth, he was a lunatic. Which do you like?

Neither was pleasing, but she suspected he was telling the truth. Not just suspected, but believed. She believed because it was probably easier to believe. And after she had climbed into bed she had fallen asleep without much fear or even anxiety.

Now she put a terrycloth bathrobe over her shirt and panties and walked to the door. She hesitated and then she unlocked it and opened it. She walked into the living room.

He was gone.

The blanket was folded on top of the couch.

"Evan," she called out.

There was no answer and she called his name out again. She walked to the kitchen and didn't see him there. *Christ,* she thought. *That was nice. Leaves without saying goodbye or a thank you. Wanker.*

She knew she should feel relieved, but she was angry. She went to the bathroom and turned on the shower. She peeled off her shirt and panties while the water heated. After she showered she wrapped a white towel around her body and walked out to the living room.

Maitland was standing in the living room.

"Christ," Sophie cried out.

"Sorry," Maitland said. He was holding cups of coffee and a small white sack. He turned around so that his back was to her.

Sophie said to his back, "What are you doing?"

"I went out to get some coffee and something to eat."

"I've got coffee here. And food."

"Well, I didn't feel comfortable rummaging around in your kitchen."

"Oh, of course, but you'll bunk in my flat while you're running from the police."

"Sorry."

Sophie stood there in her towel, her hair dripping wet, moisture running down her shoulders, looking at Maitland's back.

She sighed. "Right. Well, are they black coffees or white?"

"One of each. I'll take whatever you don't want."

"I'll take the white. There's milk in the fridge if you want some."

Maitland heard her bedroom door shut.

Later they sat at her small table in the breakfast nook sipping their coffees. Sophie was dressed now, jeans and a sweater and boots. Maitland in the clothes he was wearing the day before.

Sophie said, "You went out in the cold without a coat?"

"Yes."

"That's right," she said. "You lost it. I have a coat here if you want it."

"I doubt it would fit me."

"It would fit you. It belonged to my husband. He left it here."

"I appreciate it."

"Don't worry about it. He doesn't want it anymore. He left a lot of things here."

After a moment, Maitland said, "He left you?"

"Yes. He fell in love."

"I'm sorry."

Sophie shrugged.

Maitland said, "For what it's worth, I think he made a big mistake."

"Thanks," Sophie said. She thought back to the earlier scene, Maitland turning around so he wouldn't see her in her towel. She wasn't naked, but he had been a gentleman about it. Maybe it was all a ruse, but she couldn't help being touched by the gesture. She reminded herself that he was a stranger.

Now the stranger and she made eye contact. Briefly, then Maitland looked down at the table.

"Ah, I need to ask you a favor."

"What?"

"I wanted to see if you would drive me back to my car."

"The one you left by the rugby field?"

"Yes."

Sophie frowned. "You think it's safe to go back there?"

"I don't know. But I need the car."

"You can borrow my car."

Maitland shook his head. "You've done enough for me."

"Don't think I'm saving you. I don't want to know about it."

"But I've already told you."

"Don't tell me any more then. Perhaps it's better that way."

Maitland said, "I'm not a criminal."

"I know that."

"Do you?"

". . . I know you're not a bad man."

"I told you I'd leave in the morning. You lend me your car, it's like you're giving me an extension. You do understand that, don't you?"

"I do." Sophie slid the key to the car across the table. "Call me later, will you?"

TWENTY-SIX

Maitland liked Sophie's car. It was a white 1988 BMW 535i with a five-speed shift, one of the eighties boxy models. He drove it to the rugby field. The Ford Granada was still parked nearby, though it had a ticket on the windshield. He thought about that. London police were militant about enforcing parking regulations. If the car were towed or booted it would get back to the man he had rented it from and they would be that much closer to finding him.

Maitland drove to a pub and parked the car.

The pub had just opened and there was only one other customer. The bartender asked him what he would like to drink and Maitland said a cup of coffee. He also ordered a bowl of onion soup.

Then he called Jay Jackson, a DEA agent he used to work with when he worked narcotics.

A few rings and then Jay answered, his voice irritated when he said, "Who is this?"

"Evan."

"Evan? Goddamn it, man, do you know what time it is?"

"Oh, sorry. I forgot about the time difference."

"Time difference. Where are you?"

Shit. He didn't really want Jay to know where he was. But it was out now. Maitland said, "I'm in Europe." Which was sort of true. "I need a favor."

"What?"

"A treasury agent named Joe Roddy has been killed here and I'm a witness to it. The police want to question me about it."

"Why?"

"They think I had something to do with it."

"How do I know you didn't?"

Maitland paused, then asked, "Well, what do you think, Jay?"

"I think you're a fuck-up and I think you're in trouble and I think you're not telling me everything. But I don't think you killed a federal agent."

"I'm glad we understand each other."

"Don't ask too much, Evan."

"I won't. But I don't know anything about this agent. I don't even know where he's from. Can you find out for me?"

"I can try. What did you say his name was?"

"Joe Roddy."

"Roddy with d's or with t's?"

"I don't know. I think d's."

Jay Jackson said, "Why do I get the feeling I'm about to become a part of some international incident?"

"Because you're a paranoid government agent. You going to help me or not?"

"Yeah, I'll help you. My cell phone's not giving me a number. You got one where I can reach you?"

Maitland gave him the temporary cell number and they said goodbye.

TWENTY-SEVEN

There was one agent from the Chicago branch of the United States Treasury Department and two from the FBI who had flown in from Washington along with two from the London Legal Attaché. The agents questioned Sergeant Raines and Inspector Martin at the same time and they never asked to speak to Raines alone. The American police and the English police worked together and then the Americans left Scotland Yard and went to the American Embassy and discussed the problem among themselves. The agents from the States said they were going to check in with Washington, leaving the treasury agent alone with the two FBI agents posted to London.

The agent from Treasury was named Matt Hughes and he told the FBI agents stationed in London that Joe Roddy had never told him anything about meeting with a contact there.

One of the agents, whose name was Boone, said, "Martin and Raines said that it was Roddy's idea to meet with Maitland."

Another agent named Krewinghaus said, "And that Roddy believed Maitland had something to do with the theft of the securities." Krewinghaus looked at Hughes and said, "What did you guys have on Maitland?"

"Nothing," Hughes said. "Absolutely nothing. I never heard of him until this happened."

"Roddy never spoke about him?"

"Not once."

Agent Boone said, "We had a report on him faxed to our office this morning." Boone looked at his notes. "He used to be a cop. Chicago PD. Was investigated for the murder of a drug dealer. No criminal charges filed. He was terminated by the department, filed a grievance through the police union, went to arbitration. The arbitrator ruled that he had done nothing improper and there was no just cause for his termination and ordered the City of Chicago to reinstate him. They did and he resigned seven months later."

Krewinghaus said, "I don't see why he went to the trouble."

Hughes said, "Maybe he wanted to prove a point."

"Maybe," Krewinghaus said, "but since then, he hasn't exactly kept his nose clean. Shooting incidents, people killed."

Hughes said, "I read the file too. He claims he acted in self-defense. And no criminal charges were filed on him. And apart from that, there's no evidence he's been involved in criminal activity."

Krewinghaus said, "Chicago PD thinks he's dirty."

"Yeah, well," Hughes said, "they're not the most objective source, are they? The man beat them in arbitration."

Boone said, "You a federal agent or a criminal defense lawyer?"

Matt Hughes considered the two FBI agents. Hughes was thirty years old and both of the FBI agents had at least fifteen years on him. They had choice posts, working the Legal Attaché office at the American Embassy. Per diems and nice homes for their wives and friendly relations with Scotland Yard that maybe they didn't care to endanger.

Hughes said, "I'm a federal agent and I want to find out the truth. I presume you want the same."

Krewinghaus said, "You think Sergeant Raines is lying?"

"I didn't say that. What I'm saying is, if Maitland were a person of interest, a suspect, Joe Roddy would have told me."

Krewinghaus said, "Raines said it was Roddy's idea to meet

with Maitland and Raines is the only witness we have. Maitland's an American, from Chicago. Records show this is his first trip to London in over ten years. His passport's hardly been used. He's no jet-setter, no international traveler. Why did he come here?"

"Yeah," Boone said. "Has it occurred to you that he *is* involved in the theft of the securities, involved in trying to get them brokered here? Why else would he meet with Roddy?"

"I don't know," Hughes said. "Look, you guys didn't know Joe. Maybe he's just a subject of an investigation to you, but he was a good agent."

"Hey—"

Hughes said, "He was an uptight asshole and he wasn't the easiest guy to like, but he didn't deserve this. More to the point, he would not have kept a lead to himself. If he'd suspected Maitland of being involved in the theft, he would have told me."

Krewinghaus said, "Maybe he didn't find out until he got here. Maybe Maitland saw him and got spooked and decided to kill him."

"That's possible, sure," Hughes said. "If you believe Raines."

"Raines is a police officer," Krewinghaus said.

Hughes said, "So was Maitland."

TWENTY-EIGHT

Maitland bought a pair of binoculars at Harrod's. Then he drove back to Julian Atherton's mansion. He drove past the mansion. There was plenty of daylight left, so it wouldn't be as easy to sneak over the wall and creep up to the back as it was last time. Besides, he had a feeling the Shivers brothers or Julian had some men waiting for him this time. Maybe it would be the big bastard that drove the red Jaguar and smiled at him when he wanted to kill him. Maitland had taken out two of their men and they weren't going to allow themselves to be surprised by him again.

He parked the BMW about a half-mile away and walked back to the house that was next to Atherton's mansion. The house next door was about half the size of Atherton's, a white chalky stone house with a large yard in back. Maitland did a wide arc and came back up to a group of trees. He crouched there and took out his binoculars and he watched.

He had seen the back of Atherton's house before, though it had been dark that time. Now he saw the large windows again, the kitchen, the downstairs bathroom and the living room where the Asian girl had smacked him across the face with the riding crop.

He stayed there for forty-five minutes, watching the back of the house. During that time, he saw a big man come out of the house on the back deck and smoke a cigarette. Maitland put the binoculars on him. He recognized the man. He was the big one who had guarded the dining room at the Blue Hat Club. That is, the restaurant that was owned by the Shivers.

Maitland saw another man through the kitchen window. He thought it might have been the guy who was at the rugby club, but he wasn't sure.

Two men that he could see. Maybe there more inside or in front of the house. No sign of Julian Atherton or the Shivers brothers or the guy with the red Jag. Still, there were at least two men there and they were waiting for him in case he came.

Maitland waited some more. Maybe another half-hour passed and he saw the man in the kitchen stand up. The man was receiving someone, engaging someone. Now Maitland saw a woman. It was the woman he had seen at the rugby field. The dark-haired beauty. Maitland pressed the zoom on the binoculars.

Body language can reveal a lot. The man was smiling at her, flirting. The woman answered him with a cold, dismissive glance. Then she got something out of the refrigerator. She walked out of the kitchen and the guard shrugged his shoulders.

Maybe it meant Atherton was here. Or maybe the woman was bored, waiting for Atherton, wondering where he was and when he was going to come home.

Shit. What good would it do if Atherton was home? What would he say to him? "You're coming with me, we're going to the police." How much good had it done last time? Maitland didn't think he would try that this time. Maybe it would be easier this time, away from a crowd. Get him alone and point the gun at him and ask him, "What is this about?" See if they could work out a deal.

Yeah, Maitland thought. *Work out a deal with a guy who's trying to frame me for murder.*

Well, it was getting cold out here. He had to do something.

Maitland focused the binoculars on the kitchen again. He

had noticed something on the table when the man had stood up. Now it was revealed. It was a sawed-off shotgun.

Colin Exley went to the front of the house and looked out at the semi-circle drive. Lady Anne's Porsche was in the drive in front of Mitch's old Land Rover. No one on the front lawn or beyond. Same as it was a half-hour ago and a half-hour before that.

Exley sighed. He lowered his Sten machine gun to his side. Attached to the barrel of the machine gun was a thick silencer. A leather strap was attached to the gun so that it could be slung over the shoulder. A mercenary's weapon. Exley was bored. Ian had sent him and Mitch to watch Julian's house and watch out for the American. Ian said Julian wouldn't be there but the American might come looking for him all the same.

What Ian hadn't told Exley was that the American had killed another one of Ian's men. The other one, Marko, had had his ankle shot out. Exley had learned this from Mitch, not from Ian.

Exley told himself it would do no good to be mad at Ian. Ian could tell him whatever he wanted. The Shivers paid Exley and Mitch good money and it was always good to be on the good side of the Shivers.

But Christ, this was dull. Sitting around a big mansion with nothing to do but watch television. And Ian also hadn't told them that Julian's girlfriend was going to be here. She was a good-looking hide, but she treated Exley and Mitch like they were coal miners. Julian always had good-looking birds around him, but they were snooty. Lady Anne came from the titled aristocracy, but she was on the edge of being broke like a lot of them. Looking down her nose at Exley and Mitch, but she was a whore, no matter what you put before her name. A high-class slag.

Exley returned to the living room and sat on the couch. He set the machine gun on the cushion next to him. Then he picked up the remote control and turned on the television.

He flipped through channels, seeing news events he had already seen before. He stopped briefly on an episode of a British sitcom that had been a redoing of *Friends* then moved on; he'd never liked either version. Then back to the news . . . Prince Charles making a speech in Zimbabwe, the cloth-eared sod. He flipped to another station.

Then stopped.

He thought he had heard something.

"Mitch?"

No response.

"Mitch?"

Nothing.

Shit. Asshole had probably stepped outside for another smoke. Still . . . Exley picked up the machine gun and walked out of the living room. Through the hall and into the kitchen.

There was a television in there too. A little flat screened one on the counter. It was on and Exley thought it was funny that Mitch would be watching a woman's chat show, he must be really going ape, and the volume was louder than it had been. But then he noticed that while Mitch was still sitting at the kitchen table there was thick gray duct tape over his mouth and his shotgun wasn't on the table. Mitch's eyes had a wild, frightened look in them.

Maitland stepped out from behind the refrigerator, leveling the shotgun at Exley's body.

Maitland was about ten feet away from him. Exley had the machine gun on his right side, but Maitland was on his left.

Maitland shook his head and said, "You won't make it."

Exley remembered the man from the club. He had let him go in so he could meet with Alistair Lethbridge. Everyone knew

160

Alistair was a poof and maybe for that reason Exley hadn't thought much of this man. He seemed ordinary then. Now he had a pump-action shotgun pointed at him, his finger on the trigger.

Exley said, "You sure?"

"You bet your life," Maitland said.

Exley looked again at his cohort's eyes and then he crooked his head and Maitland knew then that the guy was making a feint and Exley twisted his body and raised the machine gun and Maitland pulled the trigger and shot Exley in the side. It broke his body as if he'd been hit with a wrecking ball and the force of it threw him against the wall, splattering blood, the machine gun clattering to the floor.

Mitch Cargill's eyes went wide as he saw it, Exley dead, the stupid sod, and the American would probably kill him next. His mouth was taped so he couldn't scream or call for help. His hands were duct taped to the back of the chair and his feet were taped to the chair legs.

Maitland took the box of shotgun shells from the counter and stuffed them in his jacket pocket. Then he turned to Mitch Cargill and said, "I'll be back."

Maitland picked up the machine gun and ran upstairs. He found the dark-haired beauty on a bed watching television. Her eyes were sleepy. Pills or booze or both. She was wearing velvet sweatpants and an orange T-shirt with a picture of Barack Obama on it.

She looked at Maitland and said, "Oh, Christ. Another one."

Maitland realized she thought he worked for Julian. He said, "Where's Julian?"

"He's not here. Who the fuck you think you are, coming in here?"

"Where's your boyfriend?"

"How do I know? Look, he's not here."

161

"When do you expect him back?"

"I have no idea."

Maitland sighed. The mission had been a bust. No Atherton and a dead man downstairs. Maitland looked at the woman again. He could force her to come with him, but she seemed pretty stoned. Probably she wouldn't be worth the trouble. Maitland lowered the machine gun to the floor and pushed it under the bed with his foot. The woman seemed not to notice.

Maitland said, "Where's your cell phone?"

"In my bag. Over there."

"What's your name?"

"Anne Halliday. Who are you?"

Maitland walked over to her purse, which was sitting in a chair. He took her cell phone out and brought it to her.

"All right, Miss Halliday," Maitland said and held up the shotgun. "I'm going to hand you the phone and you're going to call Julian and ask him where he is. You tell him I'm here and I'm afraid I'll have to shoot you."

The woman looked at him blankly for a moment. Then she said, "Oh, is that what the noise was downstairs?"

Maitland shook his head. "Make the call," he said.

She dialed the number as Maitland climbed on the bed with her and sat next to her. He put an arm around her shoulder. With the other arm he held the shotgun across his lap, the barrel pointed at her stomach.

Julian answered on the third ring.

"Hello?"

"Julian, it's me."

"Hello, luv. You at the house?"

"Yes."

"Did you have your breakfast with Siggy?"

"No. She wasn't feeling up to it."

"Oh, that's a shame. How are the lads?"

Maitland gave Anne a look of warning.

"They're all right, I suppose. I stay out of their way, they stay out of mine. How long must they stay?"

"A couple of days, no longer."

"Will you be finished with your work then?"

"Definitely."

The Lady Anne placed her fingers on Maitland's knee. She let them rest there, not making eye contact with Maitland.

She said, "Can I come see you, darling?"

"No," Julian said. "I'm afraid I'm busy at the moment."

"Just for a visit."

"It's out of the question."

Anne Halliday looked at Maitland. Maitland raised the shotgun about four inches and let it fall on her thigh. The woman gave him a full-lipped smile.

Then she said, "Julian? You're not with Fanny, are you?"

"Oh, for God's sake, Anne, don't be a bloody fool. I told you I'm working."

"But where?"

"I'm with Ian. I have to stay with him for a couple of days."

"Ian? For God's sake, why?"

"Business. Christ, what's wrong with you, asking me about such things on the phone. Look, I'll call you tomorrow."

Julian clicked off his phone. Anne Halliday turned to Maitland and said, "He hung up."

"Yeah, I heard."

"He said he was with Ian."

"I heard that too."

Anne Halliday ran her fingertips along the barrel of the sawed-off shotgun. Maitland had to stifle a laugh. The woman leaned in to kiss him. Maitland felt her lips on his. He slid his

163

hand over to her phone and took it from her. Then he slid off the bed.

She looked up at him, a pouting expression on her face. "What's wrong with you?"

Maitland said, "You like games, don't you?"

"Don't you?"

"Not today."

"What are you doing with my phone?"

Maitland dropped it into his coat pocket. "I'm going to have to borrow it for a while."

"God, you're not nice at all."

Maitland said, "What does Julian do for the Shivers?"

"I don't know. Business. Deals. I don't know. He doesn't tell me everything. Doesn't tell me anything, really. Next month, he'll be with some other trophy. What am I to him?"

"What's he to you?"

"A distraction from boredom. Don't you get bored sometimes?"

"Not that bored."

The Lady Anne frowned. She thought she was going to have some more fun. She said, "So you're leaving then?" As if Maitland had used her and was now discarding her, and not in the way she would have liked.

"Yeah."

"Well, aren't you going to tie me up or something?"

"No," Maitland said. "I don't think that will be necessary. Just stay in this room for the next hour or so and don't make any calls."

"How can I? You've taken my phone."

"I'm sorry about that."

"No, you're not."

"Well . . . a little sorry."

The Lady Anne lay back in her bed and Maitland walked

out, closing the door behind him.

In the hall he wondered if she would think to look under the bed for the machine gun. He doubted it but kept his eye on the door as he walked away.

Downstairs, he found the second man still taped to the chair but now the chair was on the floor. The man had blood from a cut on his brow where he had probably hit the ground. A tear stain on his cheek, likely from pain and the seeming futility of escape.

Maitland walked over and crouched next to him. Maitland tore the tape off his mouth.

The man gasped for breath and Maitland said, "You tried to move, didn't you?"

"Yeah."

"You should have stayed where you were. What's your name, soldier?"

"Mitch."

"You working for the Shivers, Mitch?"

"Yeah."

"Okay," Maitland said. "You see your friend over there? That was his decision, not mine. You tell every man working for the Shivers what you saw. Tell them this isn't their fight. Tell them the Shivers aren't worth dying for."

"What do I tell Ian and Ken?"

TWENTY-NINE

Kenny said, "Look here, you slag. Go back upstairs and get back in bed. We'll talk to you later."

The Lady Anne did as she was told.

Kenny Shivers was in the kitchen with Cliff Wilkinson and Mitch and three other men. Mitch had helped the three guys carry Exley's body out to a van they had parked on the lawn in the backyard. Now two of the men were cleaning Exley's blood and flesh off the walls and floors.

Mitch Cargill sat at the kitchen table smoking one cigarette after the other. Earlier the woman had come downstairs to free him from his bond after she had heard him shouting for help. Maitland had not put the duct tape back on his mouth. Mitch was grateful for this.

Mitch told Cliff and Kenny what had happened, modifying the truth at times. He told them that he had left the kitchen to use the toilet and when he came back out the American jumped him from behind and stuck a gun in his ear. Then the American took his shotgun from him and led him to the kitchen and tied him to the kitchen chair using the duct tape. He said the American put his finger to his lips and then Exley had come in and the American put his shotgun on Exley and told him to drop the machine gun. That Exley had made a move and the American pulled the trigger and cut him in half. Mitch told them what the American had said to Exley.

Kenny repeated it back to him.

"You won't make it?"

"Yeah," Mitch said. "That's what he said. He was warning him. But Exley tried him and died for it."

Kenny said, "Least he died trying, which is more than I can say for you."

Mitch Cargill's hands were shaking. He said, "Christ, Ken, I'm sorry. I swear it all happened so fast."

"You bloody fool. You let him get the jump on you. You just as well killed Exley yourself."

"It wasn't like that, I swear. He—"

"Were you sleeping? Come on now, tell me."

"I wasn't sleeping. I told you, I was in the toilet. Exley was supposed to keep an eye on the perimeter."

"What was he doing with the cow upstairs?"

"I don't know. He was up there for a minute. I tried to get away then, but I couldn't. He came back down here and Christ, Ken, I thought I was a goner when he came back, but he showed mercy—"

"Mercy?" Ken smiled.

"Yeah," Mitch said. "He said—he said this wasn't our fight. He said it was between him and you and Ian and that me and the others should stay out of it."

Kenny punched Mitch in the face, knocking him off the chair. Then Kenny kicked him again and again, Mitch trying to scoot away, Kenny still kicking him.

Cliff Wilkinson stepped in and put a restraining hand on Ken's arm. Kenny whirled on Cliff.

"Don't you fucking touch me," Kenny said.

Mitch was still on the ground, raising his voice, "He said you weren't worth dying for." Which brought him another kick.

Now the men on cleaning detail were paying attention. Mitch continued with a sudden and urgent boldness, saying, "And I asked him, I asked him, 'What do I tell Ian and Ken?' And he said, 'Tell them they should rethink their plan or they can die too.' "

Kenny pulled a pistol out of his coat pocket and shot Mitch Cargill three times in the chest. The shots boomed out in the kitchen, Mitch screaming after the first bullet but not after the second or third. One of the clean-up men dropped his mop, jumping back.

Cliff Wilkinson crouched next to Mitch. Observed him and felt for a pulse.

Cliff said, "Christ, Ken. You killed him."

"Fuck him," Kenny said. "We'll clean this up too."

There was a silence in the room. Kenny took his stare off Cliff and then looked behind at the men working on cleaning up the blood.

"What the fuck are you looking at?" Kenny said. "Get back to work, you sods."

The men started back, avoiding the mad man's hateful wrath and that was when they heard the sound of a car starting.

It was Cliff who first put it together. The woman.

Shit.

Cliff ran out of the kitchen and to the front of the house. As he got closer, he heard the Porsche engage in gear and accelerate.

By the time he got the front door open, the Porsche was halfway down the drive, the Lady Anne in it.

Cliff yelled at the back of the car, "Get back here, you bitch! Get the fuck back here!"

But the car sped up, as if she could hear him from inside. Then it was out the gate, making a left turn and gone.

THIRTY

Maitland felt better when he got to the car. He had wanted to stay a little longer and question the man in the kitchen. But a shotgun blast is loud and tends to bring attention. He had pressed his luck enough going upstairs to question the woman. He thought of it when he got to the BMW and drove away from the neighborhood. He should have played it differently. Brought the woman down to the kitchen with the other two men and questioned them together. Not exactly police procedure—a good detective usually separates his suspects—but he wasn't a policeman anymore.

And the truth was he had never been a detective. He had worked patrol and then he had transferred to narcotics and worked undercover. Posing as a mid-level drug dealer. Some of the cops at Chicago PD thought he had been undercover too long and had become a criminal himself. It wasn't true and he knew it and he wished the other cops had known it too.

Bianca had once told him he shouldn't care what other people thought of him, particularly cops. She said he was beating his head against a wall trying to win the approval of people who were not his betters. She said this was why he had done the bounty hunting work, wasting his time trying to prove something.

Maybe she was right. He wasn't sure though. He agreed with her when she said your actions shape your character and that the things you said didn't really mean much in the face of that.

He had not wanted to kill the man with the machine gun. He was ready to because he wasn't willing to sacrifice his own life to show he was better than the other man with the gun. He had told the man to drop the weapon and the man tried to use it on him and left him with no choice.

The part that bothered him now was that he had gone upstairs to see the woman *after* it was done. He had killed a man and instead of reaching for a bible and saying a prayer over the corpse he had gone upstairs to question a witness. Just like that. Pretty coldblooded. And part of him knew that it would work on the guy left in the kitchen who was still alive. Let him look at the corpse of his friend and think about what he was up against. You deal with savages and you can become a savage yourself.

Maitland left the country road and slipped the BMW into a well-trafficked street. His cell phone rang.

It was his cell phone, not the crazy woman's.

"Yeah."

"Evan, it's Jay."

"Hey. You find out anything?"

"Yeah. Joe Roddy was a Treasury agent. And Evan? He was working in the Chicago field office."

"Really?"

"Yeah, really. Evan, you sure you didn't know him?"

"I'm sure. Jay, what's going on?"

"Last week there was a theft of eight million dollars' worth of bearer bonds. The feds think Eddie Salvetti's outfit did it. They sent Roddy to London because they thought there was a chance Salvetti's people would try to unload them there."

Maitland said, "Has Salvetti got criminal connections in London?"

"I don't know. The Treasury department must have thought so. Evan, how are you involved in this?"

Maitland sighed. "I think the bonds are in London. Or they're coming."

"How would you know that?"

"Because I witnessed Ian Shivers shooting Joe Roddy. Ian Shivers killed him."

Silence on the line.

"Jay?"

"Yeah, I'm still here. Evan, what were you doing there?"

"I was tricked into meeting someone. The guy's name is Julian Atherton. He's hooked into the Shivers. Works with them. I'm not sure how or to what extent. Are you writing these names down?"

"No, I'm not writing these fucking names down. Goddamn it Evan, you going to drag me into this too?"

"Sorry."

"I mean, just what the hell do you expect me to do? Call Treasury and tell them they're going after the wrong man? I'm a DEA agent. I've got no pull at Treasury."

"I know, but—"

"Call the police and turn yourself in. Tell them what you saw. Evan, don't mess with this."

"Sorry, Jay. It's complicated. There was someone else there when Shivers killed him. A cop."

"What?"

"A police officer. Scotland Yard. He was the one that brought Roddy there."

"And the plan was to frame you for the murder."

"Yeah, that's about the size of it. But I don't think they're going to wait for the police to arrest me."

"They'll kill you first?"

"Yeah."

"Then your best bet is to go to the police. Don't you see that?"

"If I do that, they'll win."

"At least you'll be alive."

"Yeah, in a British prison. The food's bad enough on the outside."

Another pause.

Then: "What are you going to do, Evan?"

"I don't know. I'll be in touch, Jay."

He clicked off the phone before Jay Jackson could reply.

THIRTY-ONE

"Ian, you've hardly touched your supper."

"Sorry, Ma. I'm not hungry."

"Shouldn't waste food," she said.

"I know, Ma. Put it in the fridge and I'll eat it later."

Valerie Shivers picked up Ian's plate and put it in the refrigerator. She didn't cover it or put it in a sealed container. She just put the plate on the shelf next to the eggs. Then she turned to her sons and said, "Fancy some ice cream?"

Kenny said he would. Ian shook his head.

Valerie took the ice cream out of the freezer and spooned five scoops into a bowl. She put sprinkles on it and set the dish and a spoon on the table before Kenny.

"Thanks, Ma."

Valerie left the kitchen and went into the dining room. Soon the brothers heard the sound of the television.

Kenny shoveled ice cream into his mouth, noshing loudly. Ian looked at him.

Ian said, "We can't do Anne Halliday."

Kenny downed another mouthful, taking his time.

"What?"

"I said we can't kill Anne Halliday."

Kenny shrugged. "Got no choice. She's a witness."

"You fucking clod. This is not some East End tart we're talking about. This is a fucking lady."

"Lady, is she? Fancy her yourself, do you?"

173

"Shut up. She disappears and the police will be down on us like a curse from Moses. We haven't got that much protection. Besides, how are we going to get Julian to forge those certificates when we've snuffed his fucking girlfriend? And what about Melvey?"

"Julian needn't know. Nor Melvey."

"Julian'll know, you sod. How could he not know?"

"If he threatens to squeal, we do him too."

"Oh, Christ. Do him too. That's your bloody answer to everything. Bloody hell, Ken, when are you going to fucking grow up? We wouldn't be having this conversation if you hadn't have whacked Mitch. Over what?"

"He—"

"Over fucking nothing, that's what. You can't control your fucking temper and now we've got another fucking mess to deal with."

"Boys!" their mother called out. "Language."

Ian kept his attention on Kenny. "As if we didn't have enough to worry about," Ian said.

"What are you so concerned about?" Kenny said. "It's just another woman. You afraid Doreen will disapprove?"

"Leave Doreen out of it, Ken. I'm warning you."

"Don't you threaten me. Ever. You got plans to marry Doreen?"

"Yes. And I don't need your permission to do it."

A contemptuous shrug. "It's your life," Kenny said. "Do what you like."

"I can't have a wife and kids and a house in the country when I've got a brother who can't control his emotions and cuts up poofs and shoots fucking geezers anytime he likes."

"You've done your share of killing, Ian."

"And always for a reason. The way you're going, we'll both end up in Wormwood."

174

Kenny looked at his brother and said, "You're not responsible for me."

And that did it. At that moment, Ian couldn't hate him. They had had fights since they were boys. Bloody, long, bruising affairs. They still fought, though they had not exchanged blows in years. *You're not responsible for me*, Kenny says. But he was responsible. How do you turn your back on your brother? Your mirror image?

And Ian knew Kenny was right about Doreen, and maybe some other things too. Like many Englishmen, Ian Shivers was class conscious, and he longed for acceptance by the upper classes. Slag though she was, Anne Halliday was a member of that class. If they disappeared her, that world would be closed off to Ian and Doreen and their kids.

Would marriage help him escape from his brother? How do you escape kin?

Ian decided that now was not the time to discuss this. Later, he would persuade Ken that they wouldn't need to kill the Lady Anne. The woman was a pill-popping boozer, but she knew who they were and what they were.

Ian softened his expression. "Ken. Let's deal with her later. What about the American?"

THIRTY-TWO

"Who is Anne Halliday?"

Sophie set the cup of tea on the table. A white cup with a white saucer beneath. Also on the table was buttered toast and strawberry jam. She had cooked him dinner. Bacon and eggs. She said it was all she had and Maitland said it sounded great to him. It was, too. Maitland didn't think he would want the toast and jam afterward, but looking at it on the table he decided he did.

Sophie said, "Anne Halliday? Why would you ask about her?"

"I met her. Don't ask me how."

"She's upper class. Titled."

"Titled?"

"A lady. Lady Anne." Sophie sat across from him. Her cup and saucer matched his. "Don't tell me she's mixed up in this."

"I don't know that she is," Maitland said. "She is involved with Julian Atherton."

"She's a wild one. Enjoys scandal, enjoys living dangerously. Your type, I would say."

"I wouldn't." Maitland looked at the woman and she looked back at him. Maitland said, "It's getting dark out."

"It gets dark early here," Sophie said. "Are you supposed to meet with Miss Halliday?"

"No. I was hoping she'd be able to lead me to Atherton."

"Can she?"

"In a way. He's with Ian Shivers. Hiding from me, I guess.

And planning something."

"What are they planning?"

Maitland said, "You said you didn't want to know anymore."

"I know what I said."

They looked at each other again. Then Sophie said, "You brought a shotgun into my flat. I found it in the closet."

"Sorry."

"You might have at least made a better effort to hide it."

"I'm sorry. I'll go."

Maitland stood. He started to move past her and she put a hand on his arm.

Sophie said, "You can't go. Not now."

"I shouldn't have stayed this long. I haven't been thinking of you. I've only been thinking of—"

"I know what you were thinking," she said. "I'm one of the few friends you have here."

Her hand was still on his arm. Sitting before him, her blond hair resting on her brow. Maitland said, "You're my only friend here. That's why I have to leave."

"But it's changed now."

"You're right. It has changed. It's gotten worse."

"No," Sophie said. "You don't understand. I can't leave you in the breach. Not now."

"But you don't know me. You said it yourself."

"We know each other well enough. How long does it take?" She stood up and put her hands on him.

"Sophie . . ."

She leaned in and kissed him on the cheek. Maitland hesitated. She kissed him again, this time on the neck.

Maitland said, "Do you know what you're doing?"

"I know," she said. She put her hands on his shoulders and

177

kissed him on the mouth. Then she took him by the hand and led him to her bedroom.

Later, Sophie sighed and said, "Oh, you're sweet. Very sweet." She turned to him. "Feel better now?"

Maitland laughed. "Sure."

"You work fast, don't you? Your second night here and you've got me in bed."

"I don't usually work fast."

"Don't you?" Sophie touched the mark on his face. She said, "I noticed this before. What happened?"

"A woman hit me with a riding crop."

Sophie frowned. "Lady Anne?"

"No. It was this Asian woman." Maitland told her about the people he had first met at Atherton's mansion. The man being spanked, the woman slashing him across the face with the crop, the woman firing the .45 across the room.

Sophie said, "A tall, thin man?"

"Yeah. He was doped up."

"Pale-skinned, you say?"

"Very. Sickly pale."

Sophie said, "Do you know who that was?"

"No."

"That was Tony Coburn and his wife Thuy. Don't you know who they are?"

"No."

"He's a playwright. Very, very successful. He writes rock operas. You mean to tell me you never heard of him?"

"I haven't."

Sophie laughed. "She shot a gun at you?"

"She was zonked. I don't think she knew what she was doing. It surprises me to hear they would hang out with someone like Atherton."

"Atherton? They're probably friends with the Shivers. The Shivers are celebrities, you know."

"Why?"

"Oh, who knows? This is England. It's better to be talked about than not talked about."

"I don't understand it."

"You're not English. Do you have any idea how much the London papers would love that story?"

"Me getting shot at?"

"By her, yes."

"Well, like I said, I don't think she meant to shoot at me. I think she just wanted a kick."

Sophie Palmer looked at him. "And you?" she said.

Maitland said, "What do you mean?"

"Is it a kick for you? Running about with guns, shooting people."

"What do you think?"

"I think you're a very unusual man. Perhaps not a violent one. But maybe a little too . . . comfortable . . . with it."

"I see."

"I don't think you do." Sophie said, "I had a great uncle who fought in the war. He was evacuated at Dunkirk. Then he was a bombardier, flew missions over Germany, dropping bombs. He killed lots of people, though to him they were only Germans. He never talked much about it. Though once, when my mum asked him, he told her he never felt guilty about any of it. He thought her question was silly. The Germans had bombed London, you see. He thought the only moral thing to do was to kill them until they stopped trying to kill us. Then, after Germany surrendered, he was sent to Burma to fight the Japanese."

"Geez."

"Yeah. They didn't give the soldiers much rest then."

179

"Did it mess him up, doing that?"

"Not at all. He said the hard truth was that most men were not uncomfortable killing. At least, not in self-defense. He said it was no more complicated than that."

"And this attitude he had, did it repel you?"

"When I was younger, I thought he was prehistoric. A fascist. We once had an argument about Hiroshima. I told him dropping the H-bombs was an Allied war crime."

"Allied? But wasn't it the—"

"I was a college student then. I didn't know anything. Well, he did this trick on me. He asked me, in a nice but persistent way, if I would be willing to give my life for one of the lives of the Japanese that had been killed at Hiroshima. Pressed me on it and eventually I said I wouldn't. Then he said, 'But you'd be willing to sacrifice my life, though.' "

"His life?"

"Yeah. If the Americans hadn't have dropped those bombs, he would have been one of the soldiers that had to invade Japan on the ground. And would have likely perished in the doing."

"That's a clever trick."

"Yes, it was. But he wasn't, you know, a shit about it. He talked to me the way a grandpa would to a child he was fond of."

"How did it end for him?"

"The war?"

"Yeah."

"He came back from Burma and went to work for British Gas."

"Because it was done."

"Yes. Because it was done."

After a moment, Maitland asked, "What did you think of him?"

"I liked him very much. He was one of the gentlest men I've ever known."

THIRTY-THREE

A man pushed back the large sliding door to the warehouse and Cliff Wilkinson drove his red Jaguar through. The sliding door closed. The red Jag pulled to a stop next to a Ford van and a Rolls Royce. Ian and Ken Shivers stood near the Rolls. Cliff Wilkinson got out of the Jag, along with two other men. Cliff and the two men walked to the back of the Jag and opened the trunk.

Inside the trunk was Alistair Lethbridge. His hands were cuffed and his mouth was gagged by a white cotton shirt. His eyes wide with terror. Cliff pulled him out and brought him over to a chair and put him in it.

"Hello, Alistair," Ken said, his voice cheery. Like something fun was beginning.

Ian said, "Take the gag off him."

Cliff Wilkinson took the gag off.

Lethbridge gasped out his breath. His hair was mussed, his face wet with sweat and streaks of tears. His mouth hung open, his lower chin quivering. He had been hoping not to see either of the Shivers though he had feared it the moment he saw Cliff Wilkinson approach him outside the club.

Now Ken moved in front of him. Looked at him for a long awful moment. Then Kenny said, "You've been naughty."

Lethbridge said, "I don't know what you're talking about."

Lethbridge waited for the strike. Ken jumped, throwing his shoulders forward, but it was only a feint. Lethbridge cried out, frightened, and Kenny Shivers smiled that awful smile of his. The laughter of the men echoed in the empty warehouse.

Ian said, "Come now, Alistair. We know your haunts. We've been checking on you. Smitty says he saw you at the Roundy talking with an American."

Lethbridge put a quizzical look on his face. "When?"

Kenny punched him in the nose. Lethbridge's head snapped back, the momentum tipping him and the chair over. Cliff Wilkinson and another man picked Lethbridge and the chair up and put him back in his place.

Kenny said, "Take his glasses off."

Cliff Wilkinson took Lethbridge's glasses off and stuck them in his breast pocket. Kenny took a knife out of his pocket and opened up the blade.

Then Ian said, "Alistair, listen to me. Kenny here would like to cut your eye out and hold it in front of you. You won't believe he's going to do it, but he will and then you'll have to look at it with the one you got left. Now are you going to be reasonable?"

"Christ—"

"Ssshh. Listen to me: did you speak to Maitland the other night?"

"Yes."

"What did you tell him?"

"Nothing."

Ken brought the knife down in an arc, slicing open Lethbridge's cheek. Lethbridge screamed, a red stripe thickening on his face.

"That was a warning," Ian said. "Now what did you tell him?"

"He asked about Julian and about you two. He wanted to know if Julian worked for you."

"What did you tell him?"

"I told him to forget about Julian. I swear, Ian. I swear to God, I told him to forget about it."

"Did you tell him where to find Julian?"

"No!"

"He was at Julian's house. How did he know where that was?"

"I don't know. I don't."

Kenny made a gesture to Cliff. Cliff grabbed Lethbridge by the back of the hair and yanked it back. Kenny moved over him, the knife poised above the eye, ready to dig and scoop, Lethbridge screaming.

"Hold it," Ian said.

Lethbridge saw the point of the knife, an inch maybe two above his pupil. Kenny held it there.

Ian said, "Maybe there's a way you can keep the eye."

"I'll do anything you like! Please!"

"Right," Ian said. "You're going to make a call."

Ken said, "And you'd better convince."

THIRTY-FOUR

In the morning, Maitland made a pot of coffee and some toast. Sophie was still in bed. After eating the toast, he stood at the window sipping the coffee and looking out at the street, wondering what to do. That was when his cell phone rang.

"Yeah."

"Maitland. This is Alistair Lethbridge. Are you still in London?"

"Yeah. What's up?"

"I think I may be able to help you."

"Help me with what?"

"What we talked about earlier. Your situation."

"You mean the Tarenton chair?"

"No, not the chair. The other thing."

Maitland moved away from the window. Now he saw Sophie coming out of the bedroom wearing a checked bathrobe.

Maitland said, "Now you're willing to help me?"

"If I can," Lethbridge said.

"What changed your mind?"

Lethbridge said, "I don't like them anymore than you. And for some reason, I feel partly responsible for your plight."

"You are responsible for my plight. You lined me up with Atherton."

"I told you before, I didn't know it would come to this."

"And now you're all eaten up with guilt."

"Yes. I'd like a chance to put it right. But I've a selfish interest as well."

"And what would that be?"

"I don't want to go to prison for accessory to a crime."

"Are you willing to talk to the police? Tell them what you know?"

"I'd like to talk to you first. In private. Without the police."

"Will you tell the police that Atherton set me up?"

"Perhaps. But I can be implicated in this as well as you. The point is, this is a delicate matter."

"I don't know that I'd use the word delicate."

"Whatever word you like. I think we should discuss terms."

"Do you want to discuss this at your home?"

"No. There's a club in the Chelsea. The Pigeon. We can meet in an hour."

"And you'll come alone?"

"Of course."

"Why don't we say two hours? London's a big city."

A pause. Then Lethbridge said, "If you like."

Maitland clicked off the phone.

Sophie said, "Who was that?"

"Alistair Lethbridge. He wants to meet with me."

"Isn't he the one that got you in this mess?"

"Pretty much."

"You don't trust *him*, do you?"

"No."

"Then for Christ's sake, don't go. It's a trap."

"Yeah, most likely. But I've got to do something."

"Like get killed?"

"Get closer," Maitland said. "I'm tired of waiting for them to come after me."

Sophie offered to drive him to his car. He accepted, but told her she couldn't come with him to meet Lethbridge. That after she dropped him off at his car she was to go home and wait for him to call. Sophie asked, "Who do you think you are, giving me orders?" Cross with him then.

Maitland said, "All right, go wherever you like, but you're not coming with me."

"Why? Is it because you think the Shivers will be there waiting for you?"

Maitland didn't answer.

And Sophie said, "That's it, isn't it? Christ, what is the matter with you? You're going to walk right into it."

"If the Shivers have got him, they'll kill him."

"You go and they'll kill you. Call the police, have them come down there."

"They're protected by the police. I'm not."

"So you'd rather die than go to jail."

Maitland wasn't sure about that one. "I go to jail, they stay free. I'm not having that. Not after what they did."

"God," she said. "You're so . . . American."

"You going to drive me or not?"

"The offer's withdrawn," she said.

He watched as she walked into her bedroom, slamming the door behind her. Then he watched the closed door. She was something. Something to look at and hold and talk to. An uncommon woman, as tough as the country she lived in. Maybe if there was time he could explain things to her and try to get her to understand, maybe even try to get her to forgive him. She would deserve that, at least. She would deserve someone better than him, something better than this.

Maitland checked the rounds on the .45. Two left. Shit. He put the gun in the left side pocket of the overcoat he had borrowed. He went to the kitchen and found a pair of scissors in a drawer. He cut the right pocket out of the overcoat. This way he would be able to hold the stubby shotgun under the coat. He tried the coat on and walked around the apartment holding the shotgun inside. It felt comfortable to him, reminding him of the "mare's leg" sawed-off shotgun he kept in Chicago. He would need it if he was going to meet up with these folks—he had not forgotten about the man with the machine gun at Julian's house. They would be waiting for him, heavily armed. He had not liked killing the man with the machine gun, had not enjoyed it. But the man had made his decision, and you could waste time and emotion wishing it had gone another way but it wouldn't change anything. They had come after him. They had brought it to him first.

Maitland took the shotgun out from under the coat and set it on the dining room table. That was when Sophie came out of the bedroom.

She was dressed now. Blue jeans and a blue sweater. Her eyes went to the table, to the shotgun lying between the tea cups that had not been cleared away.

She said, "Planning to take that on the train with you?"

Maitland said, "I thought maybe I'd get a cab."

She shook her head at him and walked to the closet in the front hall to get her coat.

"Let's go," she said.

She drove in silence, Maitland feeling her anger. Keeping to the left, down a series of narrow streets, the houses and flats looking the same, Maitland at one point saying, "It's not so foggy today," and she didn't say a word in response.

They got to the Ford Granada, Maitland was glad that it was still there. He said so and Sophie said, "What did you expect, that it would be stolen?"

"I don't know."

"It's an old car, hardly worth stealing. You're lucky you didn't get the wheel clamped." She turned and looked at him for the

188

first time since they had gotten in her car together. She said, "I hope you know what you're doing."

"Yeah," Maitland said, "I do too."

She lifted her hand briefly, then put it back on her lap.

She said, "I suppose if I don't hear from you, it'll mean—"

"You'll hear from me. I promise."

She shook her head sadly, perhaps in fear, perhaps in pathos. "Go on," she said.

Maitland stepped out and closed the door. The white BMW hung around a few moments while he got into the Ford, and then it accelerated away and he was alone.

Maitland checked his watch. He had an hour and a half. He would have to get there early. Though he would have to make one stop on the way.

The stop was at a place called "Notions." What it sold was sex toys. The girl behind the counter looked disconcertingly young, maybe eighteen or nineteen, her hair ceramic-looking and brittle because it had been dyed too many times. She was reading a Harry Potter book and chewing gum. She glanced up at Maitland when he walked in and said "hello" and nothing more. Maitland looked around. A lot of black leather and chains and some paddles that were interesting. Maitland didn't want to spend much time there so he went straight to the girl and said, "Do you sell handcuffs?"

The girl said, "Yeah."

Maitland asked for three pairs.

He could tell her he had his own pair back in the States and that he had used them for bounty hunting work, not play, but he didn't see the point. She seemed like she didn't much care what he did with them. While she was getting them Maitland picked up three red and white bandannas.

When the girl was ringing him up, she asked, "Are you a

Man United fan?"

Maitland looked at her for a moment, wondering what she was talking about. Then he told her he wasn't.

THIRTY-FIVE

The Pigeon was on a stretch of road in a dark neighborhood with abandoned shops and some not abandoned. It was rundown and worn out and there weren't any people walking on the sidewalks in front. They had told him to come to a pub called The Pigeon because they wanted to put him at ease thinking he would be in a public place and not likely to be killed there. It wasn't like they suggested he meet Lethbridge in an alley or an abandoned drive-in movie theater, presuming they even had such things in Britain. What's the worry? You're in a bar. But Luca Brasi had been garroted to death in a bar, thinking he had fooled them when it was the other way around.

Maitland did a drive by The Pigeon, saw a pub with very small windows and he wondered about that, wondered about whether they were being clever and he was the fool for thinking he was being smarter than them. The things you could get yourself into thinking you were clever. Too clever by half, as the English would say.

Well shit, he thought. What did you expect? That there would be a huge plate-glass window where you could see Alistair Lethbridge sitting at a table, waiting with one leg folded over another?

If he walked in the front door Ken Shivers could be waiting for him in a booth, waiting with a shotgun and a few of his friends. Maybe they'd have plastic on the floor so they could roll his body up in it and put it in a trunk for his final destination.

Maitland drove a hundred yards and then some more before he turned the car around and did another slow drive-by. He didn't see anything more on the second pass. He drove to the next intersection and made a left turn. He parked the car fifty yards down the road and walked back to a diner. Behind the counter was a large black woman holding a pot of coffee. Sitting at the counter were three young men and a girl. They were laughing, enjoying themselves, one of them saying you can tell a girl from Essex is having an orgasm when she drops her chips. The black waitress looked up at Maitland with a friendly expression and asked, "Can I help you, love?" A British accent, which shouldn't have surprised him but did.

"Cup of coffee," Maitland said, then asked, "Do you have a bathroom?"

She pointed to the back of the diner and Maitland kept walking—he'd never fully stopped and given the woman much time to look at him.

Maitland walked to the back hall. Past the bathrooms there was a back door. Maitland looked to see if there was a fire alarm attached to the door. There wasn't, this being England. The door to the men's room was open. Maitland pulled it shut then went out the back door.

He closed the back door behind him. Now he was outside.

He was in an enclosed area. There was a red wood fence about eight feet high. There was no patio furniture, just a couple of trash cans and an old, rusted bicycle. There was a door in the fence, bolted from the inside.

Slowly, carefully, he opened it and stepped out.

He was in the open now. It was a gravel lot with two cars in it. One was a big blue Mercedes 500SE. The other was a vintage red Jaguar he had seen before.

Maitland's heart jumped. They were here all right. They were waiting for him.

He had known it before, had known it without knowing it and now it was confirmed and the smart thing to do was go back into the diner past the black waitress and out to his car and go. Discretion being the better part of valor and all that.

But if he left, where would he go? Back to Sophie's and then what? Ask her to drive him to the airport where he would be arrested, the corrupt police officer ready to swear evidence against him? He needed help, and Sophie couldn't get him out of this one. He needed someone who knew what was going on, someone on the inside. He had tried to get Julian Atherton and that hadn't gone well at all. Now Atherton was under the protection of the Shivers, staying at the Shivers house. Lethbridge could help him, Lethbridge knew things. Lethbridge may not have been inside, may not have been working for the Shivers, but the Shivers had him . . . maybe they had put a bullet in his head right after he had made the call to Maitland, but maybe they hadn't, maybe he was still alive and if he was still alive he would be in that pub, waiting to lure Maitland in for their trap and then probably waiting to die himself.

What did he owe Lethbridge? Probably nothing. But Lethbridge owed him plenty. It was Lethbridge who had brought him into this mess, and maybe Lethbridge could pull him out. Maitland studied the lot. It stretched out about two blocks, bordered by an "L" shape of buildings on his left and behind him. To his right there was a stone wall. Straight ahead, the back lot arced out to the road. Maitland edged against the wood fence, looked and then ran to the red Jaguar, using it for cover. He peeked over the roof of the Jaguar. Near the exit of the back lot he saw a green Peugeot. Two men in the front seat. And now he saw that it was good that he hadn't tried to come back here that way, that he hadn't tried to bring his car back here. They'd've busted him cold. But they didn't know he was back here now, didn't know that he had come through the diner. But what edge was that really? He was still only one man. What was Lethbridge to him?

Maitland moved back to the red fence, keeping his back to it. He counted the buildings and thought he determined which one was the back of The Pigeon. Each building was behind the red fence, each plot had its own red swinging door. He could not see over the fence and he hoped no one could see him. He neared the back plot of The Pigeon and stopped.

He heard movement.

A guard back there. But he couldn't see him.

Maitland stepped back. He moved back to the next plot and placed his hand on the door handle. It was an old iron handle, the sort you press down with your thumb and hold. It would creak if he was not careful and if there was a bolt on the other side of this door he was hosed.

He placed his thumb on the handle and pressed down. He heard the latch go up on the other side. Then he pushed the door inward and stepped inside.

He stilled himself and listened. Moments went by and he heard the breathing of another on the other side of the fence. Then a cough. Then, moments later, a stamping of feet. Someone back there.

Maitland picked up a rock. He hesitated a moment then threw it over the back side of the fence. He heard the movement on the other side stop. Maitland took the shotgun out of his coat. "Hello?"

A man definitely on the other side of the fence. Maitland froze. He's not talking to this side, Maitland told himself. He's pitching his voice to the back, to the place where he heard the rock land.

Maitland heard the door to the next plot open. He looked at the fence and followed the sound of the man's steps as they went. To the back door. Now opening the back door, now moving to his right, moving past the door Maitland had come in.

But the guard didn't stop at this door. He walked past it, in the direction of the diner. When he passed the door Maitland moved to it and opened it and stepped out.

He was bigger than Maitland but not much bigger. He was about ten feet in front, whirling at the sound of a man behind him, turning and looking at Maitland, a .38 revolver in his hand, startled in that moment and he thought about raising the .38 but it was just entering his mind when Maitland rushed forward and smacked him in the face with the butt of the shotgun. He went to the ground, on his back looking up, and Maitland stepped on the wrist that was attached to the revolver. The man tilted his head up and Maitland hit him again in the head and then he was out.

Maitland dragged him back into the plot and cuffed his hands around an iron pole. Then Maitland gagged his mouth with one of the red and white bandannas. He put the revolver in his coat pocket. Then he went through the man's pockets. That was where he found the keys to the Mercedes.

Kenny liked The Pigeon. It had been one of their haunts in the old days. He and Ian would come in and bully the pool players out of their money. Once one of them got mouthy with Ian and Ken had jammed a dart to its hilt between the bloke's shoulder blades. The geezer screaming and throwing his hands behind his back trying to reach it, contorting himself, Ken and Ian laughing . . . good times.

Years later they had bought the place. But it wasn't fun anymore. Ian had said it wasn't worth revamping and besides it was in a crap part of Chelsea. They used it here and there for grunt work. Punishing disloyal people and squealers. One time, they brought Georgie Parker here because Georgie had called Ken a fat poof behind his back. Georgie was drunk when he'd said it, but that hardly mattered. They had only planned to make him bleed a bit and maybe nail his fingers to the floor but when Ken showed up, Georgie got cheeky and said, "Hello, Ken. You're looking well fed." And Ken shot him in the head without preamble. Blasted temper, but what were you going to do? Sometimes it was necessary to do it quick.

That would be the way they would have to handle the American. Wait for him to come in the front door and fill him with holes. It would be nice to torture him first, but they probably wouldn't have that luxury. The American had guns and he knew how to use them. He had taken the shotgun off Mitch, the dead sod, but they still hadn't figured out where he had gotten the pistol.

The Pigeon had an oak bar on the east wall, high-backed booths on the west side. Between the booths and the bar there were circular dining tables. At the back there was a balcony, steps going up the right side. A small dining area up there, four booths for privacy and two tables. Cliff Wilkinson was on the balcony, standing back in the shadows, armed with a machine gun. There was another man with a pistol in one of the booths. Behind the bar was another man, also with a shotgun, though it was hidden under the bar. A television was on behind the bar. On it a match between Arsenal and Leeds.

There were three other men posted outside. Two in a vehicle and one behind in case the American tried to run out the back door. Ken had instructed the men in the car not to take Maitland if they saw him. They were to let him come in, then come in and stand guard at the front, penning him in. At a minimum Ken wanted to see it done. Maybe cut his ear off and stuff it in his mouth before he died.

Ken waited in the kitchen area. He would come out when he heard Lethbridge talking to the American. Surprise him.

★ ★ ★ ★ ★

How does it feel to die?

Alistair Lethbridge was wondering. He sat alone at the table, waiting and watching. He wanted to believe that they would let him live after Maitland came and they killed him. Maybe they would. Maybe they would let him live. But the memory of Kenny's knife poised above his eye kept coming back and he couldn't get rid of it. The Shivers believed he had betrayed them to Maitland. It mattered not what the truth was. If Maitland didn't come, they would kill him. If Maitland did show up, he had a chance. Maybe they would be content with Maitland's death. Maybe that would be their pound of flesh.

But maybe it wouldn't. Maybe Kenny would still want to cut his eye out. If only Ian were here. Ian was still part human. With Ian, there was a chance at reason. With Kenny, there was none. Kenny was a mad dog. Kenny was fucking bonkers. Kenny wouldn't be content just to kill the American.

Lethbridge did not like having a part in this. Maitland had done him no wrong turn. Maitland had come here for business and now he was wrapped up in this. He was arrogant, the American. Confident and quiet and sure of himself the way some Americans could be. But he was not a bad bloke and he didn't deserve to be framed for murder or killed. But . . . it was what it was. Lethbridge had to think of his own survival first.

Maitland came in through the back door. He looked through the narrow corridor and straight ahead he saw Lethbridge sitting alone at the table. Lethbridge's back was to him.

Maitland walked on quietly, the shotgun in his right hand, the barrel pointed at the ground. He walked out further. Now he saw steps ahead to his right. He looked up, wondering. . . . Now he heard the sound of a game being played on television. Maitland crept forward and now he could see the man behind

197

the bar, his attention focused on the television set.

That could be a good sign. Watching television. What a bartender would normally be doing in a bar. . . . But where were the other customers? And what about the armed guard that had been posted in back? Where was the big guy who owned the red Jag?

Leave, Maitland thought. *Go out the way you came in. Leave.*

But take Lethbridge with you.

"Alistair," Maitland said, his voice above a whisper but below speaking level.

Lethbridge turned around.

His eyes went wide upon seeing Maitland. The American right there, holding a shotgun at his side. Standing under the balcony, where Wilkinson wouldn't be able to see him.

Maitland gestured for him to come to him, mouthing the words, *"Come on."*

Lethbridge stood.

The man in the booth could not see Maitland. But he could see Lethbridge. He saw him stand. The man in the booth said, "Hey." Wanting Lethbridge to sit back down.

And Lethbridge ran.

Toward Maitland and now the man in the booth moved to the end of it and turned around the corner. He saw Maitland and Maitland saw him. The man in the booth took a Beretta pistol out of his coat and raised it and Maitland flipped the shotgun up and fired. The shot smacked into the booth and the man, sending wood flying. The man dropped his pistol and slid out on the floor. Maitland pumped another shell in the chamber and the man reached for it and Maitland fired again.

The man behind the bar pulled the shotgun out and started to raise it and Maitland turned and fired at him. An exchange of shots but the man behind the bar had fired wildly, not taking aim and he took a shot in the shoulder and face and fell back.

Maitland heard movement above him and then an eruption of machine gun fire coming through the wood floor of the balcony above him. Maitland stepped back and pointed the barrel of the shotgun up and fired. Once, then again. Maitland went further back. He saw now that Lethbridge had run out the back door.

Kenny Shivers came out of the kitchen, but now Maitland was out of his sight, having moved back into the narrow corridor. Cliff Wilkinson was coming down the stairs with the machine gun. He could see Ken and Ken could see him.

Ken pointed at the back and yelled, "That way!"

But Wilkinson hesitated. The American had just taken out two men and he could still be waiting in the corridor with a shotgun.

"Go," Ken said, pointing.

"You first, mate," Wilkinson said, not taking the time to be scared of Kenny now. Wilkinson wondered in that moment if Ken would shoot him instead but Ken moved to the edge of the corridor and peered around.

Maitland and Lethbridge were gone.

Thirty-Six

Maitland said, "Get in the car. The Mercedes. Go on, get in there."

Lethbridge ran to the Mercedes and Maitland pushed the wood door to the fence closed. He stepped back from it further and further and waited to hear someone come through the back door of the bar. Then he heard the door of the bar open and he shot at the wood door twice, blowing large holes in it.

It bought him some time and he ran to the Mercedes. He was glad he hadn't given the keys to Lethbridge. Lethbridge would have probably driven off without him. Maitland started the Mercedes and put it in gear and pressed the accelerator down, turning just as the wood door flung open and Cliff Wilkinson came out, lifting the machine gun to fire, thunking shots into the trunk of the Mercedes as it sped off to the end of the lot.

Maitland said to Lethbridge, "Get down."

Lethbridge slipped down in his seat and now Maitland saw the two men at the green Peugeot scrambling, one of them leaning across the roof of the car and Maitland considered plowing the Mercedes into the Peugeot and knocking him down but then thought better of it and pressed the accelerator down and shot into the street. The man behind the Peugeot fired twice, but missed both times.

The two men got into the Peugeot and Ken yelled at them to go after him. The driver of the Peugeot hesitated, wondering if he should wait for Ken to get in the car but the other man said, "No. Go." And they took off after the Merc.

Moments later, the red Jaguar sped out of the lot too, Cliff Wilkinson behind the wheel.

Maitland sped the Mercedes down the street. "Are you hurt?" he asked Lethbridge.

"They were going to kill me. Kenny was going to cut my eye out."

"Are you hurt?"

"No. No one shot me if that's what you're asking. I'm sorry—"

A stoplight up ahead. Three or four cars stopped, waiting. Maitland pressed the accelerator and drove around them. Swerved back in the lane when the light was behind them.

"Christ," Lethbridge said.

Maitland said, "How many men?"

"What?"

"How many men were there? I need to know."

"There were—Christ—plenty of them. Two out front, another in back. What did you do with him?"

"He'll be fine. Tell me how to get to less trafficked streets."

"What? Oh . . . go right up there. There."

Maitland said, "Put your seatbelt on."

Maitland took a right turn that angled off the busy street, the tires squealing but keeping the road. He pressed the accelerator further down. Moments later he saw the green Peugeot in the rearview mirror. When he looked again he saw the red Jag further behind.

The road was clear for a while but then it came to a busy intersection. Maitland slowed then made a right turn, sending the big Benz into a four-wheel slide, maintaining control, but just. He held on and when the car came out of the skid pushed the accelerator down again. Seeing a space ahead between two cars, he pressed on the horn and one of them moved to the left just a bit and Maitland pushed the Mercedes through, managing not to trade paint with either one of them.

He continued this for a while, maneuvering around traffic, laying on the horn when necessary, the Peugeot a few car lengths behind him doing the same. The Mercedes was a big car with a powerful engine, but the Peugeot was more nimble and could corner faster. If they were on an autobahn maybe Maitland could floor it and pull away from them. The Mercedes would probably do a steady 140, but they weren't on an autobahn, they were in a crowded city.

Maitland made another right turn, putting them on a less trafficked road, a long arc of a road, the Peugeot keeping with them and that was when the police car swept out behind them, slipping between the Peugeot and the Jaguar.

Inside the Jag, Wilkinson cursed and let off the accelerator. The police car pulled away from him, the coppers inside speeding after the Peugeot and the Mercedes.

Maitland saw it in the rearview mirror, the Jag fading back, but the police car pulling up on both of them, the sirens blaring. He debated pulling over. He would be caught by the police and arrested, but now he had Lethbridge with him and he would rather face the police than Shivers' henchmen.

But then he saw something else: the Peugeot lifting off, slowing and now the police car pulled up next to the Peugeot.

No, Maitland thought. And then it was happening. The police car falling into the trap and the Peugeot leaning in and then pushing, moving it forward at an angle, the police trying to stop the car but it was too late, the police car piling into a parked car, the front end of the police car biting in and taking hold, the police car spinning around and then flipping over as the Peugeot sped away.

The men in the green Peugeot grinned at their victory. They kept coming.

A half-mile later, there were shots.

The first couple went wild. Then one went into the trunk and another shattered the back window of the Mercedes. Maitland made a left turn in front of oncoming traffic. Cars braked and screeched and Maitland continued. The Peugeot followed.

Soon they were out of residential neighborhoods and near the main railway lines of central London. There were a series of branching tunnels underneath. The passages were narrow, graffiti on the stone walls rushing by.

In the Peugeot, the passenger dialed Cliff Wilkinson's number on his cell phone, letting him know where they were.

Maitland was glad to be away from the residential areas, but he didn't like these tunnels either. They were narrow and dangerous and he didn't know quite how to get out. He had to keep the speed up to keep away from the armed men in the Peugeot but there was always the possibility that a truck would come out of one of the intersections in the tunnel and block his path. Or that he would slam into it and be killed in the impact. He thought about something like that happening and then something like that did happen—a car nosed out of one of the intersecting passages and Maitland laid on the horn and the car scooted out of the way and Maitland floored it again, the Peugeot having gained on him, now bumping the back of the Mercedes and Maitland lifted his foot off the gas and then stabbed the brakes and the Peugeot hit the back of them again only this time not expecting it and Maitland pressed the accelerator again and put some distance between them.

The road curved and then curved some more, too much, and the Mercedes scraped up against a wall, sending sparks, and Maitland pulled it back into the center line. Then the road seemed to curve the other way—an S—and it was better that time and then the road straightened out and then they were out of the tunnel, on a lot bordering some warehouses and Maitland had to step on the brakes and crank the wheel to avoid hitting a dumpster, circling the big Benz in that small area and then the Peugeot came out too, also braking and circling and then the Mercedes came to a complete stop and Maitland put the gear in reverse and backed the Mercedes into the Peugeot, T-boning it. Maitland shifted the gear to forward, getting a few feet away before backing the Mercedes up and smacking it into the Peugeot again, harder this time.

Maitland put it in drive and took off.

The men in the Peugeot saw the Mercedes disappear around the corner. The passenger reached into the back seat for a machine pistol. They would get closer this time and pump rounds into the Mercedes' windshield.

The Peugeot moved forward. It made a left turn at the corner. Then it was in a matrix of warehouse buildings. The driver of the Peugeot moved fast but not too fast—the American would be stuck in here somewhere. They came to intersections and looked both ways. The Peugeot making a right turn and then the next left.

Up ahead, there was a T-intersection. The driver of the Peugeot debated whether he should make the left turn there or go forward. The passenger seemed to read his mind. He motioned forward with his hand. In his other hand was a machine pistol. When they reached the T, the passenger looked to his left and heard the Mercedes engine's roar at the same time he saw the car.

The Mercedes hit the passenger side of the Peugeot square, slammed it forward and smashed it against the wall.

Maitland unlatched his seatbelt and got out. He held the shotgun on the Peugeot as he approached it. When he got close he saw the men inside were not in good shape. The passenger had not been wearing his seatbelt and he had been knocked into the back of the car. The driver had been wearing his seatbelt. He was slumped over. He lifted his head, groaning. Looked over and saw Maitland pointing the shotgun at him.

"Christ," the driver said. "Please don't. All I did was drive."

"And what about when you caught me? What were going to do then?"

". . . please . . ."

Maitland shook his head. "I told one of your associates, this isn't your fight."

"I work for Ian and Ken. . . . Anyway . . . you killed Mitch . . . at Julian's . . ."

"Mitch? I didn't kill him."

"Ken and Cliff . . . they say . . . you did."

"I didn't. They must have. After I left."

"Should I believe you . . . over them?"

"If you've got any sense." Maitland lowered the shotgun. He said, "If I see you again, I will kill you. Stay out of this."

The Mercedes was totaled.

Maitland told Lethbridge to get out of the car and they hurried away. Lethbridge said they could board a train a few hundred yards from here and Maitland said that was probably a good idea. They reached a stone bridge a few minutes later, steps going up to a street. Lethbridge went ahead of Maitland and Maitland started to walk up after him and that was when Maitland saw the red Jag coming under the bridge, accelerating toward them.

THIRTY-SEVEN

"Run," Maitland said, hurrying up behind Lethbridge. Lethbridge turned and saw Cliff Wilkinson's Jag and he hurried up the steps, Maitland behind him, pushing him now. Lethbridge reached the top and turned and got down behind the brick wall. Maitland turned and saw Wilkinson get out of the car, holding the machine gun, coming to the foot of the steps. The shotgun was empty now. Maitland pulled out the .45 and fired twice. It slowed Wilkinson, made him stop and hesitate and that gave time Maitland time to reach the top of the steps and take cover behind the wall.

Wilkinson stepped back and took cover behind the wall under the overpass.

Now the .45 was out of ammunition too. Maitland reached into his pocket and found the .38 revolver he had taken off the man behind the pub. A five-shot gun.

Maitland peered over the wall, didn't see anyone. He could see the front of the red Jag. Four shots left now. Wilkinson peered around and Maitland fired the revolver at him. It missed him, but hit the car.

Maitland took the box of shells out of his pocket and started putting them in the shotgun. then heard a voice call out.

"Hey! Don't fuck up the car, you sod!"

Maitland called back, "Next one's for you, brother."

"Fine! But don't shoot the fucking car! It's vintage!"

Maitland actually smiled. He said, "Throw out that machine

206

gun and I won't shoot the car."

"Forget it."

Maitland leaned over and shot another round into the front of the car. He tried to hit the tire, but it was impossible to do it at this distance with a snubnose revolver. Three shots left now.

"Don't!"

"Hey," Maitland said. "What are you doing here anyway? Are the Shivers worth dying for?"

"You're the one that's had it, mate."

"There are a couple of your men by those warehouses and they're banged up pretty bad. Why don't you go check on them?"

"Fuck 'em."

"Hey, they're your men."

"They knew what they were signing up for."

"Yeah? Do you?"

"You're a dead man, Maitland. If it isn't today, it'll be tomorrow."

"Why not make it today then?" Maitland said. "Or do you like it better when they can't shoot back?"

Silence.

And now Maitland thought about this man. Standing above a balcony earlier, waiting for Maitland to come into a bar so he could shoot him in the back. Now he was here and he was thinking things over. Now he knew his two men weren't going to show up to help him out. He had a machine gun and it was one against one. How did the man like those odds?

Maitland said, "Walk away and we both live. I'd say that's a fair offer."

"No way."

"Remember your man Mitch? I left him at Julian's alive and then you guys came along and killed him. And you've been telling people that I did it. How come?"

"Fuck him. He was a coward."

207

"Coward? What about you? I'll bet he was still tied to the chair when you and Shivers killed him. That's how you'd like it."

"Fuck you."

Maitland moved forward. Further along the wall so that he was closer to being more above Wilkinson. Maitland did not know how many rounds he had put in the shotgun. He racked one now, hoping it made a loud noise.

"I'm losing patience," Maitland said, prodding him some more. "Throw down that gun or use it."

Maitland looked over the wall. He could see the shadow of the man standing beneath the bridge.

Maitland said, "I'm going to count to five. One. Two. Three—"

Wilkinson stepped out on four, whirling around the corner and firing up the steps. But Maitland wasn't at the top of the steps anymore, he was above Wilkinson. Maitland shot him in the chest, the force of it knocking Wilkinson back, his arms flinging out and he went down to the bottom, the surprised expression frozen on his death face.

Maitland wiped the shotgun clean of prints, then deposited it in a trashcan.

On the train, Lethbridge looked at him for a long while, looked at him as if were someone different. Not the American antiques dealer he had met a few short days and a lifetime ago, but a savage, cold-blooded and determined.

Maitland returned his look. "What?"

Lethbridge shook his head, as if the episode had not been so much horrifying as it was distasteful. "I don't know how you could do something like that."

"You mean defend myself? And you?"

"But you drew him out. You pushed him. We could have run."

"He would have followed and shot us both in the back."

"You don't know that."

"He said it himself," Maitland said. "If not today, then tomorrow. Were you listening?"

"I was, unfortunately."

"Would you have rather stayed with him?"

"No."

"Then don't second-guess me. I'm not in the mood for it." Maitland was angry at the Englishman. He didn't like being judged in these circumstances. He knew the Englishman was an ingrate and a snob, but a small part of him still feared the judgment was due.

Then Lethbridge said, "All right," and made a conciliatory gesture with his body. "I suppose I should be thankful."

"You can if you want," Maitland said, "but it's not going to clear your account with me. I haven't forgotten that you're the one who got me into this."

"You want me to go to the police?"

"Maybe. But I don't trust you to tell them the truth."

"Under the circumstances, I don't blame you," Lethbridge said. "But you're forgetting that now the Shivers want me killed as well. And this." Lethbridge gestured to the large cut on his face. "So perhaps I've my own motive for cooperating with the police."

"And telling them what?"

"As much as I know."

"That may not be enough." *Or maybe too much,* Maitland thought. He didn't like the idea of British police knowing he had shot people, even if it was in self-defense. The British weren't fond of guns and maybe not all that crazy about self-defense either. It was their country and he was a guest in it. "Listen," Maitland said, "the Shivers have someone at Scotland Yard on their payroll."

"Could be anyone," Lethbridge said.

"I only know one," Maitland said. "His first name is Bill."
Lethbridge thought a moment. Then he said, "Bill Raines."

"Big man, with a mustache?"

"Yes. That's him. He's a DS. That's Detective-Sergeant."

Maitland said, "He was there when Ian killed the American agent. Ian tried to get him to shoot me afterward. How well do you know him?"

"Not well. I've seen him with Ken and Ian and Julian at the club. Other places as well. Yes . . . I've long suspected that Bill was a bent copper. Like most."

"Most aren't, actually," Maitland said and gave Lethbridge a look. Maitland was no longer a police officer, and he'd met his share of crooked ones. Yet he still felt a kinship with law enforcement even if the goodwill wasn't generally returned. Jay Jackson, Julie Ciskowski, other law enforcement officers he'd worked with and respected. He didn't hold the many responsible for the sins of a few. But he was pissed off at this Bill Raines, now that he'd put a name to the face.

Maitland said, "What do you know about stolen securities?"

"Nothing," Lethbridge said.

"You sure? Some bearer bonds were stolen in Chicago. The American government thinks they might be moved to London. That's why the Treasury agent was here."

"I don't know anything about it. I told you before, I'm not included in such things."

Maitland said, "What about Julian?"

Lethbridge sighed. Then he said, "He might be."

"I think he is," Maitland said. "Tell me why you think he is."

"Julian's the fixer. That's what they call him. 'The Fixer.' He's good with documents, papers. He knows financial instruments."

"Does he know how to forge stock certificates?"

"I suspect he would."

The train slowed to a stop. Maitland said, "Is there a place you can hide?"

"Yes."

"Lose yourself then," Maitland said. "But give me a cell number."

Lethbridge wrote it down.

Maitland stood and moved to the doors.

Lethbridge said, "But what will you do?"

"I'll be in touch," Maitland said. "Stay hidden."

THIRTY-EIGHT

"This is Special Agent Hughes, United States Treasury."

"Agent Hughes?"

"Yes. Who is this?"

"Are you investigating the murder of Agent Joe Roddy."

"Yeah. Who is this?"

"A witness."

"Identify yourself."

"Evan Maitland. I'm from Chicago."

Matt Hughes leaned back in his chair. In his Chicago office, he would have a switch on his telephone that would activate a tape-recording device. But he didn't have one in this London office. He fumbled in his jacket pocket for his own portable recorder.

Hughes said, "We've been looking for you."

"Why is that?" Maitland said.

"You tell me."

"You're looking for me because a Scotland Yard police officer has accused me of shooting Joe Roddy to death. Am I right?"

Hughes saw the telephone number of the caller on his own telephone. Hughes wrote it down. Hughes said, "Why don't you come in, we'll discuss it. Get your side of it."

"You can get my side of it now. Ian Shivers killed Roddy. I saw him do it. Sergeant Bill Raines of Scotland Yard was there. He was the one who brought Roddy there. Check Sergeant

Raines out. He's on the Shivers' payroll. You know who they are?"

"I know," Hughes said and signaled a secretary to come to his desk. "Do you?"

"I do now," Maitland said. "I didn't before I got to London."

The secretary came to Hughes's desk. Hughes gave her the written number, covered the phone and told her to get a location for it, stat.

Then Hughes said, "Maybe you did and you're having trouble remembering."

Maitland said, "You want to read me *Miranda?*"

"I don't have to," Hughes said. "We're on foreign soil."

"Was Roddy your friend?"

"Yes."

"You want to get the man who killed your friend or do you want to find someone to hang it on?"

"What do you think?"

"I don't know you," Maitland said. "I don't know what to think."

After a few moments, Hughes said, "Scotland Yard thinks you're here to help unload some stolen securities. What do you say?"

"I'm here to buy a chair for a client in New York. His name is Max Glendenning. Call him and he'll tell you why I'm here. I deal in furniture, friend."

"Some people say you dealt in narcotics."

"One or two *claimed* I did. I testified at a hearing and so did they. An arbitrator believed me."

"Arbitrators can be fooled."

"So can federal agents." Maitland said, "Let me ask you something: you worked with Roddy, did he ever tell you I was a suspect?"

Silence.

And Maitland said, "Well?"

"No," Hughes said. "He didn't."

"Think about that," Maitland said. "And watch out for Sergeant Raines. He set Roddy up to be killed, and he'd do it to you too."

The secretary returned and placed a yellow pad before Hughes. Written on the pad was, *Public telephone—Victoria Station.*

Hughes said, "Maitland. Let's say I believe you. I'll need you to testify against Shivers and Raines. I'll need to see you to talk about it. You can't manage this on your own."

"I don't know that you do believe me," Maitland said. "Not yet anyway. I think you need time to think about it."

"I'm ordering you to come in. Do you hear me?"

"I have to go," Maitland said. "You've traced the call by now."

"Maitland. Listen to me—"

"Check on Raines. I'll call you in two hours."

"Maitland."

The line went dead.

Agent Boone brought two coffees from the concession stand and handed one to Agent Krewinghaus. They stood near the pay phone from which Maitland had made the call. Maitland was gone now, as they had expected him to be. At least a dozen trains had come and gone in the past half hour and there was no point in stamping feet over it.

Victoria Station was crowded as usual. The sound of train engines and doors opening and closing echoing under the high rafters and rows of blue and white skylights. Commuters moved through the concourse, a mere part of the eighty million passengers that passed through the station each year. The surveillance cameras showed a number of people using the telephone, more than one of them wearing a hat. Nothing conclusive.

Hughes could feel the weight of the judgment of these two agents, both of them older than him and heavier with weight and so-called experience. Hughes knew they were waiting for him to apologize or shrug his shoulders and say he was doing the best he could under the circumstances, but he wasn't going to give them the satisfaction.

Finally, it was Boone who asked, "Well, what now?" Directing the question at the young agent.

Hughes almost said he didn't know. But he stopped himself, knowing he could not look indecisive in front of these two. They were waiting for him to make a misstep, waiting to shake their heads at the inexperienced neophyte.

Hughes said, "We question Raines."

"We don't have the authority," Krewinghaus said.

"He's been questioned," Boone said.

Hughes asked, "What if he lied?"

The older agents groaned and Hughes said, "We have two witnesses to that incident. Two known witnesses. Maitland and Raines. Raines said Maitland killed Joe. That he killed him and then he ran. What if Maitland did? What if Maitland did kill Roddy? If he had done that, don't you think he would have killed Raines too? Come on. Think about it. If he had the ass to kill an American federal agent in cold blood, why would he leave a witness? Why wouldn't he have just popped Raines *before* he took off?"

"Raines is a police officer," Krewinghaus said.

Hughes said, "Raines said he wasn't armed."

"I meant," Krewinghaus said, "Raines is a cop. He's entitled to—"

"He's not entitled to a pass," Hughes said. "Not if he had a hand in this. Anyway, Maitland was a police officer too."

"Was," Krewinghaus said. "He was fired."

"He was not fired."

"He *was.*"

"Okay, technically he was. But he filed a grievance through the police union and he won it. He testified and his accusers testified and the arbitrator ruled in his favor. He was reinstated with full back pay. By that decision, the termination was expunged."

"Bullshit," Boone said.

"It's not bullshit. It's the law." Hughes looked from Boone to Krewinghaus. He said, "Look, if you think I give a damn about Maitland, you're wrong. It's Joe I'm concerned about. Maitland says Ian Shivers killed Joe, not him. If that's true, I don't want Shivers getting away with it. Or Raines."

"Maitland's got a motive to lie," Krewinghaus said.

"As would Raines. If he's dirty."

"Yeah, *if,*" Krewinghaus said. "You trust Maitland over Raines?"

"I don't trust either one of them," Hughes said. "One of them is lying. But I don't think we know enough to say it's not Raines."

"Speculation," Boone said.

"It's not speculation," Hughes said. "It's a reasonable, objective examination of the evidence. You still haven't explained to me why Maitland would kill Roddy and leave Raines alive."

"How should I know?" Boone said, wanting to end the conversation.

Hughes said, "We're investigating the death of an American treasury agent. I think it's something you would want to know."

Boone said, "Who do you think you are? You got here, what, yesterday? We've been stationed here for years."

"Maybe that's part of the problem," Hughes said.

"Now what the hell—"

Hughes cut Boone off, saying, "We've got a dead federal agent. An American killed overseas. Roddy didn't say anything to me about Maitland. Nothing. If he thought Maitland was a suspect or even a lead, he would have told me. I know he would have. Now you're asking me to back off. You're *demanding* that I take the word of one British policeman that an American citizen killed him and leave it that. Now why is that? Because you think it would be bad politics? Because you don't want to step on the toes of Scotland Yard? Well, I'm sorry gentlemen, but that's not a good enough reason."

"Gentlemen?" Boone said. "Where do you get off, patronizing us? Huh? We have no evidence that Bill Raines is in the pay of the Shivers brothers. Nothing except the word of our prime suspect, who has every reason to lie about it."

There was a silence. Then Agent Krewinghaus said, "Well, that's because we really haven't looked." Krewinghaus looked at Boone, then at Hughes.

"Jesus," Boone said, disgusted. Shook his head and walked away.

Krewinghaus said to Hughes, "I think we may have a problem approaching Raines directly. He's not obligated to talk to us. And his DCI may try to protect him, tell us he's already given a statement."

"So we shouldn't even try?" Hughes's blood was still up and it showed. He wanted to believe he had won over Krewinghaus, but Krewinghaus could be playing him too.

Krewinghaus said, "I didn't say that, Matt. I'm just warning you what we're in for. We're still on their turf."

THIRTY-NINE

Ken said, "He was dead when I got there. Blown apart with a shotgun."

Ian said, "What about the other two?"

"They're in the hospital. One of them's got a concussion. The other a broken collarbone." Ken shrugged.

They were seated near the bar of their restaurant. A delivery man came in pushing a hand cart stacked with cases of beer. He began pulling the cases off and unloading them.

Ian said, "So that makes seven of our men he's taken out. Not counting the one you killed."

Ken didn't respond.

Ian said, "DeGiusti's hit England today. We're supposed to meet him at the Ambassador Hotel tonight. Me, you, Julian."

"You don't need me there."

"DeGiusti's expecting you there. A show of respect. Besides, there's nearly five million dollars on the table."

"We've unfinished business."

"It's money, Ken."

"He knocked off Cliff, or have you forgotten that?"

Ian said, "And what was Cliff doing there alone? Why weren't you there with him?"

"He left before I could get into his car. He wanted him for himself."

"You say Maitland came in through the back. How did that happen?"

"We had Eddie posted back there. He got the jump on him."

"And let him live."

Ken said, "It was your plan too, Ian."

"Shut up. Now Alistair's free and he'll grass to the coppers."

"No he won't," Ken said. "Not that poof."

"Maybe."

"Yeah, maybe." Ken Shivers cocked his head. "How come it's all right to take out Alistair but not Lady Anne?"

Ian didn't answer him. He just looked at him and said, "The Ambassador Hotel, tonight. You're coming. We do this together."

"And after that?"

"After that, we find the American and we kill him."

"Alistair too?"

"Anyone who helped him, yes," Ian said. "People have got to know, don't they?"

Ken Shivers smiled.

FORTY

Maitland switched trains in Wembley and took another back to South London. The Ford Granada was where he left it. He got in the car and started the drive back to Sophie's apartment.

Halfway there, he stopped and thought about what he was doing. Did he want to go back to Sophie's when this thing still wasn't resolved? He had just called a cop and more or less confessed that he was there when the federal agent was murdered. Yes, there was that. And there were the men he had taken off the Shivers payroll. Could he bring that back to her? Could he explain why he had killed the man driving the Jaguar? Even Lethbridge had been chilled by that. Would Sophie understand? He had given them all a choice, including Cliff Wilkinson. Throw down your gun and surrender. But the man chose to come after him. It was his choice.

But Lethbridge said that Maitland had taunted him. And Lethbridge had been right about that. Maitland had called him a punk, had questioned his manhood, had made him act. Should he feel guilty about that?

He didn't feel guilty. Not exactly. But he knew now he had acted in anger and that wasn't common for him. It wasn't good to kill in anger, but he had and there was no erasing it. He could go back to the woman's apartment and tell her he was sorry for burdening her and tell her he could fall in love with her and that he needed her and they could make love but it still wouldn't purge him of his sin. He could understand it now, understand why he had done it. Wilkinson and the Shivers had killed a man he had left tied to a chair. Killed him and put the blame on Maitland.

But there was blood on Maitland's hands for that murder too. Maitland had tied him to the chair and told him to tell the Shivers "they should rethink their plan or they can die too."

A threat. And he had used a man tied in a chair to deliver that threat. Now Maitland knew the man had delivered that message and died for it. They had literally killed the messenger. And if Maitland had been thinking more about natural consequences than his own personal beef he would have seen it coming and kept his mouth shut.

It was different when a man came at you with a gun. It was justified then and if your nature was cold enough you could tell yourself it was that simple. But could you justify risking a man's life just so you could deliver a message? Just so you could deliver an insult? Wasting a man's life over words.

He had done that. He had not intended to do it, but it had happened and he had caused it. And instead of looking at himself, he had put it on Cliff Wilkinson and killed him for it. Maybe Lethbridge thought he was no better than the Shivers. Maybe Sophie would think that too.

Now he wondered if it would make him feel better to track down the Shivers brothers and kill them too. Would he "win" if he did? Or would he simply be putting himself at their level? Savage, brutal, efficient.

Was there a better way of handling this?

There had to be. . . . Didn't there?

Maitland checked his coat pocket. He still had Anne Halliday's cell phone.

FORTY-ONE

The bartender gave Ronald Martin a warm greeting. "Hello, Inspector. The usual?"

"Yeah. How are you, Dennis?"

"Can't complain."

"How's your boy?"

"Still in Afghanistan, fighting the fourth war. You know how it is. Had him home for Christmas, though."

"That's nice."

The bartender set a pint before the Inspector. The Inspector took a sip and looked up at the television behind the bar. Blair, the former prime minister, was being interviewed by some twit on the BBC. Blair saying the usual rubbish. Inspector Martin was not fond of Tony Blair. He held him responsible for putting Dennis's son and a whole lot of other sons of England in Iraq and Afghanistan, fighting somebody else's senseless war. Unlike the Americans, the British had dealt with the Afghans before and it had never gone well. Inspector Martin thought the British should have known better.

Martin felt a presence next to him. The bartender acknowledged the newcomer and asked him would he fancy a drink. The customer said Diet Coke and right away Martin knew it was an American.

Inspector Martin turned and looked at the man and didn't attempt to hide a frown.

Agent Hughes said, "How are you doing?"

"Well, thank you," Martin said. He looked ahead, giving the American agent his profile.

"It sure gets cold here," Hughes said. "It's a wet cold. I guess I'm not used to it."

Martin said, "Maybe you'll feel better when you go home."

"Yeah, maybe," Hughes said. "But I can't leave until I get this thing resolved."

Inspector Martin shrugged. The bartender set a Diet Coke in front of Agent Hughes.

Hughes said, "You know, Joe Roddy was a pain in the ass. He went to the University of Michigan law school. You know where that is? No, I suppose you don't. It's one of our top law schools, and Joe thought since he'd graduated from there he was smarter than everyone else. He never said that, but you could tell he *thought* that. He and I started at Treasury at about the same time, and it was tough because the older agents resented him for thinking he knew how to do their jobs better than they knew. You know how that can be."

Inspector Martin said nothing.

"But he was getting better. Once he figured out he didn't have to always be the smartest guy in the room, he started becoming a pretty good agent. And people started to like him. Well, maybe not like him, he was difficult to like. But they respected him and that was the important thing."

Martin glanced at Hughes.

Hughes said, "He deserved that respect."

"I'm sure he did," Martin said.

"Do you know he had a wife and two little kids? They meant everything to him. When I go back to the States, I'm taking his body with me."

Inspector Martin looked at him again.

Hughes said, "What do I tell his wife and kids when I get there?"

"Tell them the truth," the Inspector said.

"And what is that?"

Inspector Martin said, "We've answered your questions. We've given statements."

"I know," Hughes said. "I think yours was truthful."

There was a silence, Inspector Martin waiting for the American to add something. The American didn't.

Martin put a fierce expression on his face. "What are you saying?"

"I spoke with Maitland," Hughes said. "His story's different than Sergeant Raines."

"You've got Maitland?"

"No. He called me. We're still looking for him."

"If he's still loose, what are you doing here?"

"I think you know."

"No, I don't know, Mr. Hughes. But if you're suggesting what I think you are, you're getting ready to have your face smashed in."

A moment passed and the American agent did not get down off his stool. He said, "Let me ask you something. Before Roddy met with Maitland, did he say anything to you about it?"

"No."

"Did Raines?"

Silence and then Hughes said, "He didn't, did he? Doesn't that bother you? Doesn't it bother you that they would meet with an alleged suspect and not tell you about it?"

"I'm sure Bill had his reasons."

"What reasons?"

"I don't know. He forgot."

"Whose idea was it to meet with Maitland?"

"Roddy's. Your people's."

"Is that what Bill told you?"

"Yes. And it's the truth."

Hughes shook his head. "No. Joe would have told me. He was the sort to clear everything. He was very thorough, very by the book."

"You're not putting this on Scotland Yard, mate. It's just bloody not going to happen."

"I'm not trying to." Hughes leaned in. "Maitland was in London to buy a chair. To buy an antique. His story checks out."

"That's because he had the cover story ready. *Before* he came."

"Maybe. But his story makes sense. The more I examine this, the more his version of the facts makes sense. The more I examine this, the more Sergeant Raines's story doesn't make sense. There are too many holes."

"Get out of here."

"No." Hughes said, "You know what else Maitland said? He said Ian Shivers killed Joe. Shot him and then tried to get Raines to kill Maitland. Maitland was the fall guy."

"I'm warning you—"

"No, I'm warning *you*," Hughes said. "It's looking more and more like Raines is an accessory to murder. You want to protect him, I can't stop you. But my suspicion is you have doubts about him too. But if he's dirty, all of Scotland Yard isn't going to come to his defense. And then where will you be?"

"Fuck off."

Hughes stood up and stepped away. He set a couple of pounds on the bar and said, "Give it some thought, Martin. But remember, if he's bent, it's not him you're helping, it's the Shivers."

FORTY-TWO

Lady Anne Halliday lived in a house in Hampstead, north of London. An idyllic village perched on a ridge, overlooking the modern city. Maitland drove by the front of the house that matched the address he had found on the reverse look-up using her phone number. It was a tall and narrow house on a Georgian street. The house had six windows, including a small one in the center on the third floor. If she saw him through any one of those windows approaching the house she might call Julian Atherton or even Ian Shivers himself. Or she might get turned on and let him in. Or she might do both. She was crazy and beautiful and maybe even a little lonely.

Maitland dialed information and soon got the number of a local flower shop. He asked them to send a dozen roses to Anne Halliday's address and said he would pay twenty pounds extra if they could deliver them within one hour.

An hour and twelve minutes later, an old Austin mini-van pulled up in front of the house. A young man got out of the van holding a dozen roses. He went to the front door and rang the bell.

Anne Halliday came to the door and answered it. She wore black sweats and a velour maroon top and house slippers. Dressed like Victoria Beckham now, the upper classes aping the new-money lower classes. She read the card, which only said, *An Admirer,* shook her head and dismissed the delivery boy.

The delivery boy drove the flower truck away and Maitland

approached the door.

Anne Halliday opened it and Maitland stepped in.

She stepped back and looked at him for a moment. Then she said, "Oh, it's you," showing neither disappointment nor elation. Then a little curiosity came into her expression and she said, "How did you find me?"

"I still have your phone."

"Oh, yes. Can I have that back?"

"Sure. I may need you to help me, though."

"I see. Have you still got your gun?"

"Just a small one."

"Hmmm," she said, giving him an up and down look. "Look, you can't stay long. I've got some friends coming over."

"What friends?"

"Not Julian, if that's what you're wondering."

"Where is Julian now?"

"I don't know. I still haven't seen him. Not since I saw you. Perhaps I shall never see him again."

"You may be right about that," Maitland said. "What happened after I left his house?"

"Oh? Let's see . . . some other men came over and there was some shooting and I left. Are you my admirer?"

"Yeah. You said there was some shooting?"

"Yes."

"And they let you leave after that?"

"Well, I didn't exactly wait and ask. I thought it would be an opportune time to leave."

Maitland said, "Haven't you worried about what might happen since then?"

"Not especially."

"Did Ian Shivers come to Julian's house after I left?"

"No. Ken did. Ken and a couple of other men. I'm not afraid of Kenny."

"You should be. He's a murderer."

"Oh, what he does is his business. I didn't leave because I thought they would harm me. I just left because I was tired of the scene. Ken would never harm me."

"You don't know him."

"I know him better than you. You see, the Shivers are typical working class. They make a cockney show of things, but like all British, they want to be upper class. Ian, especially. As for Ken, well, he's too fond of Uncle Ernie to do anything to me."

"Uncle Ernie?"

"Yes. Uncle Ernie. Ernest Halliday." She smiled. "You know, Lord Melvey."

Maitland shook his head. "I'm not from here. So you're going to have to explain that."

Anne Halliday sighed. "Well, let's at least have a drink."

They sat a table in her kitchen and she drank wine and he sipped from a glass of water with not enough ice. She explained the connection to him without any shame or embarrassment. Told him that Ken and Lord Melvey shared an attraction for young men, the ideal age being between eighteen and twenty. Old Uncle Ernie liked his chickens, she said. But what with being titled and a member of the House of Lords and all, he had to exercise a certain amount of discretion. Ken lined him up with boys. In exchange, Uncle Ernie gave him whatever protection he could at the London courts.

Maitland said, "You uncle, does he have much influence at Scotland Yard?"

"Oh, I don't know all the details," Anne said. "I suppose he has some. But it's not all about influence, you know. Uncle Ernie likes Kenny. And as I told you before, the Shivers like being close to aristocracy."

Maitland said, "I must say, I find your nonchalance . . ."

"Shocking?" Anne Halliday smiled. "Well, you Americans are too parochial."

"Yeah, maybe that's it," Maitland said.

The Lady Anne missed the sarcastic note and said, "In any event, I must tell you if you plan to do battle with the Shivers, you're making a huge mistake."

"Maybe so," Maitland said. "But I must tell you that I think they're going to kill you. And eventually they'll go after your Uncle Ernie too. You may find them amusing, but they're brutal killers. Men like that don't reach a plateau and then decide they're going to stop committing murder. They keep on doing it. For them, it's the first resort. *That's* their business."

"And what about you?"

"I just sell furniture."

"You killed a man at Julian's."

"He was trying to kill me."

"I see," she said. "And you want to persuade me that I'm next."

"Lady, I don't think I can persuade you of anything. But I'm going to warn you to leave town for a few days. Until this thing dies down."

"How, exactly, will it die down?"

"They're going to answer for their crimes this time. They murdered an American cop. And the American government will make them answer for it. Regardless of how much pull your uncle has."

"Have faith in your government, do you?"

"Once in a while." He tried to look convinced when he said it. *Once in a while* sounded better than *I have no other choice.*

Anne Halliday said, "So you came here to do me an act of kindness."

"Not exactly," Maitland said. "Julian and the Shivers are going to be meeting with some people from Chicago to negotiate the trade of some stolen securities. That's why you haven't seen Julian for a couple of days. I need to know where and when they're meeting."

"How would I know?"

"I think you can find out."

"Perhaps I could. Or perhaps I could just telephone Julian and tell him you're here."

"You could at that. Then maybe we'll see Ken and Ian and a few of their men and maybe they won't cut your face up before they kill you."

"Maybe they'll just kill you. Are you willing to bet your life?"

"It's on the table."

She downed the red wine left in her glass, not spilling a drop of it, then set it down and looked at him and shook her head.

"You're either very brave or very stupid," she said. "I've never had much admiration for either trait. But you aren't a bore. And you've got a certain rough, frontier way about you that I like. Who knows? It might even be fun, helping out a man in need."

"You'd be helping us both," Maitland said.

"I'm not even sure *you* believe that," Lady Anne said. "But what the hell? You only live once."

Maitland considered this woman. *You only live once.* What was she? An alcoholic? A deviant neurotic? Yes and yes, but that didn't explain her. Not completely. A lady who seemed to feel no remorse over the murder of people around her, no disgust at the associations she made or her uncle made. She lived in probably the most beautiful neighborhood he'd ever seen in an ideal village in an ideal country. She had been born into money and icy good looks and maybe even quite of bit of smarts and she was unencumbered by shame or guilt. He felt pity for her, but he was afraid of her too. He needed her help and she seemed to know it.

FORTY-THREE

Like Sophie Palmer's uncle, Ronald Martin's father had also been a soldier in the Second World War. Martin senior's experiences were an influence in Martin junior's worldview and upbringing. Inspector Martin's father, like many British soldiers, was very critical of American soldiers. He thought they were incompetent and poorly trained and loud-mouthed braggarts to boot. He would freely and harshly abuse anyone who dared suggest that the Americans had bailed out England, reminding them in strong, clear terms that the Battle of Britain had taken place *before* the Japanese bombed Pearl Harbor and brought the Yanks into the action. England was a tough little island that had not been successfully invaded in a thousand years. Ronald Martin's father was rather typical of working-class Englishmen of his time, sure of himself and his country and defiantly prejudiced against all others.

Ronald Martin had inherited much of his father's sensibilities. He believed the England he loved was quickly disappearing, thanks to the likes of men like Tony Blair. He thought there was too much capitulation to the Muslims. He was vehemently opposed to Britain's entry into the European Community, hostile to the notion of being ruled by a cadre of unelected French and German officials sitting in Brussels. And he didn't much like Americans either.

When he had met Joe Roddy, he had taken an instant dislike to him. He thought Roddy was young and stupid and far too sure of himself. He resented Roddy for telling them how he, the super Federal Agent from the States, was going to bring down Ken and Ian Shivers. Show the English how it was done. Bloody Lone Ranger coming to their rescue.

And now there was another American federal agent here, leaning on him, telling him one of his best friends was bent.

Why?

To protect another American. An ex-Chicago policeman who'd left law enforcement under an ethical cloud. Agent Hughes said that Maitland was innocent and Bill Raines was a crook. American good, the British bad.

But Matthew Hughes concerned Inspector Martin in a way that Joe Roddy had not. Martin had thought Roddy was a fool. When he first met Hughes, he thought, *another one.* But now he was changing his mind. Hughes, like Roddy, was confident of himself. But Hughes was smarter and the things he was saying made sense.

What Inspector Martin did not tell Hughes was that he had his own doubts about Bill before Hughes came to him. Before Hughes came to London, Martin had wondered why Maitland would kill Roddy and leave Bill alive. Martin had thought Roddy was such an uptight little twit, he would not have neglected to tell them about any and all leads he had. In Martin's mind, most Americans were incapable of keeping their mouths shut and were forever anxious to show you how smart and informed they were and Roddy would be no exception. If Roddy had known that Maitland was in London and was involved with the stolen securities, he would have told Martin. If anything, just to make a favorable impression. Why would he seek to impress Bill with this information and not him?

And why would Bill go along with Roddy to meet this Maitland without first notifying Martin?

There was that and something more. Like most police officers at the Yard and many other Brits, Martin and Raines had often complained about the skyrocketing costs of living in London. London had become a city for the rich and the super-rich and who could argue? Yet in the last couple of years, Martin had started to sense that Bill's complaints were feigned or half-hearted. Last year, Martin was surprised to learn that Bill's daughter had taken a holiday in the Italian Riviera. That had to have cost around three thousand pounds. Then there was the time he had seen Bill's wife driving a late model Range Rover. Not brand spanking new, but new enough. Martin had asked Bill what the payments were and Bill had said they paid cash, adding that his wife had inherited some money.

What was he to do then? Call Bill's wife and see if that was true? Do you do that to a friend? Wouldn't that act alone constitute a betrayal?

No. Don't call Bill's wife. Talk with *Bill*. Tell him what the federal agent said. Tell him and let him say why it wasn't true. That like Martin, he believed the Shivers brothers were wicked, savage men and he would never do anything to help them. Bring it out in the open and get this thing straightened out.

Inspector Martin called Bill Raines on the cell phone. Raines didn't answer. Martin did not leave a message. What he did was drive back to HQ to see if Raines was still at his desk. But when he reached the parking lot, he saw Raines pulling out of the lot in his red Jeep Cherokee.

Martin wondered why Raines had not answered his call. Martin thought, *Call him again.* But then turned his own vehicle around and followed him. Like that the decision had been made.

FORTY-FOUR

Anne Halliday called Julian from her home phone. She put on a show, telling him she was still angry with him for leaving her alone at the house in Surrey with nothing to do and these bloody criminal friends of his. Julian tried to get tough with her, telling her he was very busy, but she continued to lean on him and soon he gave in, telling her he was sorry and he missed her and he would make it up to her sometime next week. Anne Halliday said she demanded to see him tonight or she would get on a plane to Switzerland first thing tomorrow and do God knows what naughty, deranged things when she got there. Julian again said it was out of the question, but he would probably be able to come around to her place sometime after midnight if she insisted on being such a damned nuisance about it. Anne Halliday said, "Where are you going first?"

"I'll tell you later," Julian said and hung up.

The Lady Anne turned to Maitland. "He hung up."

"Yeah, I know."

"I'm sorry, but as you can see, I did try."

"You did."

"He's up to something, though. That I can tell. He said he would be able to come here after midnight." The Lady Anne smiled at him. "Would you like to wait for him here?"

"No," Maitland said. "Do you think he'll conduct his business at the Shivers' club?"

"Oh, no." The woman paused. "Julian owns a small hotel in

Golders Green. It's called the Ambassador. He grew up in that neighborhood. It's not much of a hotel. Could use a lot of work, actually. But it has sentimental value for him. It's near the Crematorium."

"Does he ever do business there?"

"Sometimes. It's rather low key. Well, we can go look at it if you like. Or we can wait here."

"Let's go look."

Golders Green is a relatively quiet section of Greater London. There are only a handful of pubs in the area. The Ambassador was a nine-story hotel approximately ten minutes' walk from where the railway bridge crossed Finchley Road. The hotel itself seemed quiet and nondescript. A handful of windows had light in them and by eight P.M. most of those were off.

At eight twenty-seven P.M., a van pulled up to the front of the hotel and three men got out. Two of the men carried suitcases. The third man, whose name was Vincent DeGiusti, did not carry any bags. DeGiusti was a tall, handsome man with dark hair going gray at the temples. He had snuck into England by way of a cargo freighter from Hamburg, Germany. He was tired and in a poor mood, still feeling some of the effects of seasickness. His bodyguards were European, one of them Italian, the other a paid hand from the Reeperbahn district of Hamburg. The German spoke better English than the Italian. Both of the bodyguards were armed with submachine guns.

The Shivers had two guards in the lobby of the hotel. A phone call was placed and DeGiusti and his guards were on the narrow elevator going up to the top floor. There were another two guards on the ninth floor. The door to the last room at the end of the hall opened and Kenny Shivers stepped out. He smiled and called out "Vince" and spread his arms. He and DeGiusti embraced.

"How are you, Ken?" DeGiusti said.

"Lovely," Kenny said. "Have a nice trip?"

"Fucking awful. But it had to be done."

"Never much liked the sea, myself," Kenny said. "All that rolling about. How's Eddie?"

"Eddie's good." DeGiusti smiled. "Your brother here?"

"With bells on his toes. Come on in, have a drink and let's get down to business."

DeGiusti embraced Ian in the hotel room. They exchanged greetings and took a seat on the couch. DeGiusti was introduced to Julian the Fixer. The suitcases were opened and they began their work.

Anne said, "Told you it was quiet."

They were in the Ford Granada, Maitland behind the wheel. He had driven past the hotel and saw that it was dark and unwelcoming. It was winter and perhaps there wouldn't be much business but it didn't look like it encouraged business at any time of the year. Maitland looked at the hotel and wondered if it looked back at him. There was light coming from the lobby through a narrow pair of glass doors. An English hotel, unconcerned with friendly ergonomics. Maitland watched and didn't say anything.

"Well?" the Lady Anne said.

Maitland sighed. "Maybe there's something going on there. I'm going to check it out."

"Do you want me to come with you?"

"No. I'd like you to go home."

"Trust me, do you?"

"No. But I don't want you around here. It might be dangerous." Maitland turned to look at her. He said, "You are afraid of them, aren't you?"

Anne Halliday looked out the car window. "I don't know,"

she said. "Perhaps. At Julian's house, Ken told me to get back in his room and called me a slag. It pissed me off, him talking to me like that. But there was something in the way he said it, it frightened me. I tried to convince myself he wouldn't do anything to me because of Uncle Ernie, but . . . when he gets angry, there's no controlling him. I think he's mad. That thing you said about him cutting up my face . . ."

"I'm sorry I said that."

"No, you're not. Besides, you're right. I do know about him. That's the sad thing. I know better."

Maitland said, "Things will be okay."

Anne Halliday placed her hand on his cheek. "Oh, maybe," she said, sounding like she'd like to believe it. "Thank you."

"For what?"

"For being a gentleman."

She opened the door and got out. Maitland watched her walk down the street. She hailed a taxi and then she was gone.

Maitland got out of the car and walked away from the hotel. A hundred yards away he crossed the street and walked back. He passed in front of the glass doors and saw a clerk standing behind the front desk and another man standing near the elevator. When he did a second pass, he saw another man sitting on the couch. Neither of the men looked soft or old or poor or even pedestrian. One of them wore a jacket and the other wore an overcoat, both of which would have been adequate for hiding a gun.

So maybe they were working for the Shivers and maybe they were just two guys who happened to be hanging around the lobby of a quiet hotel in Golders Green. Maitland looked across the street at where he had left the Ford. He could walk back and get back in it and drive away and forget about this until another day and start looking for a place to live in England under an assumed name, but then he saw light reflect off the car, the car now in the glare of approaching headlights. Maitland moved away from the hotel and into the shadows and he saw the Jeep Cherokee turn into the hotel lot. A man got out of the Jeep and walked in the front entrance. When the man was in the light Maitland saw it was Bill Raines.

That was when he decided to call Special Agent Hughes.

The desk agent reached Matthew Hughes on his cell phone and told him there was an Evan Maitland on the phone and did he want to speak to him? Hughes was in his hotel room, the television on mute, and he got out of bed and was looking for his shoes when he said yes.

Then he heard the familiar voice.

"Hughes?"

"Yeah, Maitland. Where are you?"

"I'm at the Ambassador Hotel in Golders Green. I have reason to believe the Shivers are on the top floor. I just saw Sergeant Raines go in. I think your thieves are here. The ones from Chicago."

"Did you see them?"

"No."

"You didn't see them?"

"Look, they're here. The Shivers and Sergeant Raines. It's the proof you've been looking for. I've just told you where I am."

"How do you know DeGiusti's there?"

"I don't. I have a reasonable suspicion. Very reasonable. Hughes, call in your men and come get these guys."

"Where are you now?"

"I'm outside the hotel."

"And where are they?"

"They're on the ninth floor. The top floor. Something important is going down."

"Stay right there. Do not go into the hotel. Do you hear me? Do not go into the hotel."

"I'm not planning to. I want you guys to finish this."

"We'll be right there."

"I'll be waiting," Maitland said. "I'll surrender myself to you when you get here. Only you. Not Scotland Yard, okay?"

"Okay."

Maitland hung up the phone. That was when he heard movement behind him. He was starting to turn when the nightstick took him in the kidneys and he gasped and fell to the ground.

FORTY-FIVE

Inspector Martin reached into Maitland's jacket and took the .38 out. Then he stood Maitland up and turned him around and pushed him against a wall.

Inspector Martin said, "You're Maitland."

Maitland exhaled twice, his breath coming back to him. Looking now at the sad-faced cop he'd seen outside his hotel a couple of days ago. The cop who'd been with Sergeant Raines.

"Yeah," Maitland said. "Who are you?"

"Inspector Martin, Scotland Yard. What are you doing here?"

"What are *you* doing here?"

"I'm asking the questions, governor. You're carrying an unlicensed weapon. Stiff penalty for that in our country."

"You working for the Shivers too?"

The inspector eyed him for a moment. The gun still held on him. Maitland looked at the gun and he looked at the man holding it. The man's features were getting more visible now and Maitland took a chance, saying, "Your man Raines is here. But you already know that, don't you? I know he's dirty—"

"You mind your mouth."

"I said, I know he's dirty. You, I don't know."

Inspector Martin said, "I think you're trying to be clever. You still haven't answered my question."

Maitland said, "The Shivers are up on the ninth floor. I think they're meeting with Salvetti's people from Chicago, I think they're exchanging those stolen securities. I think Raines is in

240

on it too. I think that's why he's here."

"And what proof do you have?"

"I saw Ian Shivers shoot and kill the American agent. I saw it. After he did it, he tried to get Raines to kill me and claim self-defense. I was set up."

"That's your story."

"I called Agent Hughes. He's on his way here. If I had killed Roddy, why would I do that? Why would I call the police on myself?"

"You're lying."

"I'm not lying. Raines is working for them. If you're here, you're working for them too. Unless . . . unless you're checking on Raines yourself."

"I'm a police officer."

"Then arrest me." Maitland studied him again. "But that's not why you came here, is it? You didn't know I'd be here. You *are* following Raines."

"Shut up."

"If you're working for the Shivers, you would've killed me by now. You'd have your own gun to do it."

"Maybe I'll take you up there myself. Get this thing straightened out."

"You do that, you'll get us both killed. I told you, the feds are on their way. Let them handle it and then we'll get it straightened out."

The inspector stepped back and gestured with his head. "Let's go."

"Martin, there are armed men in the lobby of that hotel. Don't take us in there."

"I said let's go." Inspector Martin got behind Maitland and shoved him. They got closer to the front doors of the hotel.

"Martin, don't do this."

The inspector pushed him again, the gun leveled at Maitland's

James Patrick Hunt

back. They got closer to the front doors and then they were in the small lobby.

There was an arrangement of shabby furniture. A green felt couch and two sitting chairs, old magazines on a table.

The two guards were on the other side of the furniture. They were chatting with Bill Raines, the body language friendly and familiar. Raines looked over at Maitland and Inspector Martin. Maitland stepped to the inspector's side. The two officers from Scotland Yard exchanged looks and Maitland knew that Raines knew he was busted.

For it was in their faces and neither one of them could hide it. Inspector Martin feeling a disappointment and disgust at this betrayal. Shocked, but not really that surprised. His worst fears confirmed. Sergeant Raines looking back at him, ashamed and knowing no matter what explanation he came up with, it wouldn't be good enough.

Raines said, "Ronnie . . . ?"

Martin said, "Ah, Christ. Bill."

Now Martin had the gun pointed at Raines.

Sergeant Raines laughed. An unpleasant laugh, showing fear and embarrassment. Raines said, "Come on, Ronnie. There's your man. He killed the American."

One of the bodyguards looked at the other. The other bodyguard started to open his jacket.

Martin said, "Put your hands on your head, Bill."

Raines made another attempt to laugh. "You must be joking."

"Do it, Bill. I'm asking you."

"I'm your best friend. You'd take the word of this murderer over me?"

That was when Maitland yelled, "Martin!" And pointed to one of the bodyguards pulling a sawed-off shotgun out of his coat. The man raised it as Inspector Martin turned and fired

242

the .38 twice, both shots taking the man in the chest. The shotgun discharging into the ground. Martin saw Raines move, reach into his coat and he turned on Raines as Raines pulled a pistol out of his jacket and they exchanged gunfire, one shot from each and then another and both men fell back.

Maitland dropped to the ground near Martin, the chair and part of the couch giving them some cover. He saw a blood spot forming on Martin's white shirt, now spreading out. The .38 now lying on the ground. Maitland remembered there had only been three shots left in the revolver. He grabbed the shotgun from the dead bodyguard and instead of standing up and shooting he scrambled like a crab to the other side of the couch on his elbows and knees, conscious that there was still another man possibly with a gun and he heard a shot coming from a pistol punching into the chair and then another shot and then Maitland got around the couch and stood up and fired a shotgun blast into the second guard and brought him down.

Maitland hurried over to the second guard and pulled the pistol out of his hand and dropped it in his jacket pocket. Both of the guards were dead and a quick examination of Sergeant Raines confirmed that he was too.

Maitland looked over at the desk clerk. He was holding his hands up. "Don't shoot me."

"Get out of here," Maitland said.

Maitland walked over to Inspector Martin.

He was still alive, but it didn't look good. A wound below the chest and it was a mess. Martin struggled and then said, "Bill?"

"He's dead. I'm sorry."

"I killed him, didn't I?"

Maitland said, "He would have killed you."

Martin groaned. Tears rolling down his cheeks, his face cold and clammy. He was fighting shock.

Maitland said, "I'm going to have to move you. Behind the counter."

"Why?"

"Because they're coming."

From the top floor, the first pops sounded muffled and distant. They stopped and they listened, all of them wondering if it was gunfire and then they heard the shotgun blast and they knew.

It was DeGiusti who seemed the most displeased. He looked first at Ian Shivers. Ian looked back at him and then looked away and started giving orders to his men, telling them to get downstairs and check it out.

Kenny let one of the hall guards in and the guard said, "It's coming from downstairs."

Kenny said, "You and Jonesy, take the lift down."

DeGiusti kept his focus on Ian. DeGiusti said, "What is this?"

Ian said, "We'll handle it."

DeGiusti said, "You said you had police protection. Now what the fuck is going on?"

"We do. Don't get your knickers in a twist."

"Ian—"

"Just sit tight." Ian turned to say something to Kenny but Kenny was gone, leaving Ian alone with the American gangster and his two bodyguards.

Maitland couldn't find a towel behind the counter but he did find that the desk clerk had left his cloth windbreaker. Maitland folded it twice and placed it on the inspector's chest.

"Can you hold it there?" Maitland said.

"Yes," Martin said. "Were you . . . were you really set up? . . . You can tell me now . . . I won't be around . . ."

"I was set up. And you will be around. I'm going to need you as a witness."

Inspector Martin managed to smile. "You're a mercenary bastard."

"I just sell furniture."

"Wouldn't that be funny if that's all you did?" Martin inhaled and exhaled twice. Then he said, "You better get out of here."

Maitland shook his head. "If they find you, they'll kill you."

The inspector said, "I'm not your friend. I may not help you at all."

"Right," Maitland said. "Look, I'm going to have to leave you here for a while. But I'm not leaving the hotel." Maitland handed him the pistol he'd taken off Raines. "If one of Shivers' men finds you here, use this."

The inspector took the pistol and held it over the windbreaker that was on his chest. Inspector Martin said, "Maybe you—"

"Be quiet," Maitland said. "Don't make a sound until the police get here."

Then he was gone.

Maitland ran to the corner on the other side of the elevator. He had the Glock .40 in his coat pocket that he had taken off the bodyguard. The bodies of three dead men were in the lobby and when the men stepped off the elevator they would be pre-occupied with the sight. That would be when Maitland would have them. They could turn and shoot, but he would only have his gun arm and a little bit of his body exposed and they would have to be quick and good to get him.

The elevator doors opened and Maitland heard a man say, "Jesus Christ." And then they stepped out without any hesitation, the first one holding an Uzi submachine gun. Maitland hesitated, thinking there might be a second one too, and he didn't want him getting back in the elevator for cover.

There was a second one and he was holding a pistol. He came out and the elevator door closed behind him.

Maitland raised the Glock and said, "Drop the weapons."

The man with the Uzi turned and raised the machine gun and Maitland shot him in the head. The second man dropped his pistol.

"Don't," he said.

"Out the front door," Maitland said. "Go."

The man moved past the lobby furniture, got to the doors and burst through them running.

Maitland walked over to the corpse with a bullet in his head. The man was definitely dead but Maitland kicked the Uzi away from him anyway. Maitland looked over at the other side of the lobby. At the stairwell. The door was closed and he looked at it, concerned that another man was behind it. He tensed, raising his gun, and debated approaching the door and wondered if it would be better to wait. That was when the elevator door opened right behind him and Kenny Shivers stepped out and rushed him with a knife.

Maitland started to raise the gun but Shivers hit him hard and knocked him to the ground and then Kenny was on top of him, using his weight. Kenny Shivers was not a huge man but Maitland was surprised at his strength and speed. Maitland held Kenny's right hand with his left, keeping him from plunging his knife into his chest. Maitland still had the gun in his right hand but Kenny had that hand pinned to the ground. Kenny's weight was on him and Maitland made the mistake of looking him in the eye and he saw nothing there but cold, empty steel. A killing machine. Maitland feared what Shivers would do and then Shivers did it, moving forward and placing his knee on Maitland's right wrist, pinning it to the ground and now Kenny had two hands free to use the knife to press down into Maitland's eye, Maitland only having his left hand to hold him off, but Shivers was stronger than he was, the point of the knife getting closer . . .

"Kenny," a voice said.

Shivers looked up, a hanging moment, and then Inspector Martin fired and shot Ken Shivers in the face. Shivers jolted up and Martin fired again, this time taking him in the chest.

DiGiusti said to his guards, "Pack it up."

Ian said, "What are you doing?"

But the Italian bodyguard was already putting the securities back in the suitcases, taking some paper out of Julian's hand and putting it in the case with the rest.

"Vince," Ian said. "Don't do this."

"Sorry, Ian," DeGiusti said. "I don't like what I'm hearing."

Ian said, "We had an agreement." He moved toward the American gangster. The German bodyguard stepped between them.

"We're done," DeGiusti said. "Goodbye."

Ian followed them out the door and down the hall. Julian went to the door but stayed there. Ian walking behind DeGiusti and his two armed guards carrying eight million dollars on them, eight million dollars going to the elevator and out of his life. Ian trying to control his anger, knowing he couldn't shoot Vince DeGiusti and two mercenaries on his tab. Ian pleading now, but trying to make it sound like good reason.

Then DeGiusti and his men were on the elevator, DeGiusti facing him briefly before the doors closed, DeGiusti shaking his head at him and saying, "Some other time, Ian." And that was that.

Ian Shivers looked at the closed doors for a moment. He heard the elevator car descend. Then he turned and looked at Julian who was looking down the hall past him. That was when Ian turned and saw Maitland standing at the other end.

Ian stared at him for a few moments.

Ian had a gun in his coat pocket, but his hands were not in

his pockets. Maitland held a pistol at his side, the barrel pointed down.

Maitland said, "Things didn't work out, huh?"

Ian said. "I should have known it was you, causing that ruckus downstairs."

Maitland lifted the pistol, gesturing it to Julian. "You," Maitland said, "step out into the hall. There. Put your back against the wall. Now sit down."

Julian Atherton did as he was told.

Ian Shivers stared at the American for a while. Then he said, "Well, what you have got in mind now?"

Maitland said, "I'm taking both of you downstairs and turning you over to the police."

"Are you now? Just like that?"

"Yeah."

Another silence as Ian stared at Maitland and Maitland thought about him then. He was getting a look from the British gangster that was supposed to terrify, the gangster used to getting his way—using terror and violence and murder to do it. A cold-eyed killer, unencumbered by conscience. But Ian Shivers was alone now.

Maitland said, "You want to draw on me, now's the time."

Ian stared at him for a moment, wondering how long it would take to stick his hand in his pocket, not pull the pistol out but just get his finger on the trigger, lift and shoot him through the pocket. Ian's hand itched as he thought about it.

And Maitland said, "I'm ready when you are."

Maitland held his steady look and he thought he saw Ian twitch. So Maitland pushed him a little more, saying, "Come on. Maybe you'll make it."

There was a moment and Ian looked into the eyes of the American's and saw a coldness that he thought matched his own. And the moment passed. Ian smiled and lifted his hands above his head.

"Maybe I would have," Ian said. "But there'll be another time."

"No," Maitland said. "That was it, sunshine. Put your hands against the wall."

Riding down in the elevator, Maitland stood behind the two men. Both of them had their hands cuffed behind their backs.

Julian said, "I told you we should have left him out of this."

Ian said, "Julian, shut your fucking gob."

FORTY-SIX

There were about a dozen members of Scotland Yard's CO19 Division, all of them pointing high-powered rifles at the men getting off the elevator. Maitland put the guns on the floor and stepped out with his hands on his head. Ian saw Ken's body in front of the elevator and his very person seemed to crumble. He dropped next to Ken, shaking with emotion. He had about a minute of grief before the police officers closed in on him.

Later, while waiting in remand for trial, Ian told a friend that he would have rather been with Kenny in prison than to be without him on the outside. At his trial, the press noted that Ian looked like he had aged fifteen years. Spectators wondered if he would live much longer. It seemed a part of him had died and the rest of him was trying to catch up.

Evan Maitland was placed in handcuffs by CO19 and placed into the back of one of the ARV vehicles. It was Agent Matthew Hughes who got him out.

Hughes had the cuffs taken off. Maitland rubbed his wrists and said, "Are you Hughes?"

"Yeah." Hughes held up a paper cup, steam coming out of the top. "It's coffee, not tea."

"Thanks." Maitland took it, gave it a sip. "How's Martin?"

"He's in stable condition. Says you saved his life."

"It was actually the other way around."

"More than you know," Hughes said. "He confirms that

Raines was working for Shivers. Which I guess puts you in the clear."

"Good."

"It puts you in the clear for the murder of Joe Roddy. Not for the other shit you've done here."

"Like what?"

"Using firearms, to begin with."

Maitland raised a hand. "Fifth Amendment."

Hughes smiled. "I told you before, you're not in the States."

"Yeah, you told me. Was Roddy your friend?"

"Yeah. He was a good man."

"I'm sorry."

Hughes shook his head, sighed. "It's not your fault. We shouldn't have sent him over here alone."

Maitland watched the police lead Ian Shivers to a car, his head ducking as he got in. Maitland said, "Are you going to help me out of this?"

"Yeah," Hughes said. "I'll help you."

FORTY-SEVEN

About thirty-six hours later, Sophie Palmer drove him to the airport. Maitland checked his bags and then saw that he had about a half hour left before he needed to board the plane.

"Will you have a cup of coffee with me?"

Sophie Palmer said she would.

He was uncomfortable sitting at the table with her, paper cups of coffee before them. She had made him breakfast earlier and he had even had a cup of tea. He never had gotten to like it. He wanted to leave London and England and get in the air and go to sleep and wake up later to see the gray, snow-dusted cityscape of Chicago. He feared that Sophie might mistake his relief.

He said, "I want to thank you for everything. I don't think I would have made it without you."

Sophie said, "I just gave you a place to stay."

"More than that. I needed a friend."

She frowned. "Don't call a woman a friend after you've shagged her. They might think you're taking them for granted."

"I hope I haven't."

"You haven't. Perhaps." She said, "I suppose you won't come back here anytime soon."

"I don't know."

"I think you do." She put her hand on his. "But it's all right, though. No regrets."

"No," Maitland said. "None."

The desk attendant called out the flight number for boarding. Maitland stood up and Sophie walked with him to the gate. On the way there, she touched his hand and said, "Evan?"

"Yes?"

"About the Lady Anne."

"What about her?"

"Her uncle, Lord Melvey."

"Yeah."

"Did it ever occur to you that he was the one who wanted to sell the Tarenton chair?"

Maitland stopped.

The desk attendant announced that they were now boarding first class. People got out of their chairs and began to move to the gate.

Sophie said, "After all, if she was involved with Julian Atherton, it's possible that that's how Atherton knew about the chair. Because it belongs to Melvey. And he's exactly the sort who would want to conduct the sale discreetly."

A passenger stuffed his paperback into his book bag and slung it over his shoulder, then walked over to the boarding line.

"It is what you came here for," Sophie said. "What do you think?"

Maitland said, "Oh, hell."

ABOUT THE AUTHOR

James Patrick Hunt was born in Surrey, England, in 1964. He is the author of *Maitland, Maitland Under Siege, Maitland's Reply, Before They Make You Run, The Betrayers, Goodbye Sister Disco, The Assailant, The Silent Places,* and *Bridger.* He resides in Tulsa, Oklahoma, where he writes and practices law.